REINCARNATION AND LOST TREASURE

Terry Fraser

PublishAmerica
Baltimore

INTRODUCTION

This book is dedicated to all adventurers out there who have truly had adventures, also to those who are just starting out on the long and exciting journey of life as they would like it, and finally, to those who haven't chosen in which direction they wish to point their inquisitive journey to, or have not as yet had the proof of what they would truly like to believe in.

To all of you, I will take this opportunity to enlighten your way, based entirely on my own personal experience in this complex, but beautiful and gracious world that we do live in.

THREE RULES OF LIFE

Number one rule – "Always follow your heart," as your personal well-being and happiness should always come first.

Number two rule – "Always look after your health to the best of your ability," without it you have nothing.

Number three rule – "Treat all humans with respect and common courtesy," unless they prove themselves unworthy of it.

STORY CHARACTERS

To the following people, I truly thank graciously, for without them, these adventures that I am about to share with you would not have existed.

Mr. Bill Mcphee
Mr. Guy Simcoe
Miss Maggie Lightfoot
Miss Conchita Mountain
Mr. Donnie Morningstar
Mr. Ali Recinos
Mrs. Viola Recinos
Mr. Hank Smythe

Also, I must thank the next level of energy, as it also played a starring role in much of this story, the spirit world is all around us, comrades—to enter all you have to do is truly believe.

And never fear the unseen forces as they are going to guide, and shape your life in the pattern that it was indeed planned by our, "Great Creator of Forces."

I ask you now to put your feet in my shoes for a few hours, and enjoy these true adventures as much as I did.

Best regards
Terry Fraser.

CHAPTER ONE

MY FIRST GLIMPSE INTO REINCARNATION

Reincarnation is a subject that I think we have all had thoughts about. I do realize that there is the believer and the none believer. Also there is the skeptic, who remains somewhere in between. His belief will only be strengthened by contact with this subject. Or he will remain a weak skeptic, or a none believer, due to no interest in the subject, or no contact, either by accident, or planned activity in this direction.

My own personal interest in reincarnation first came to me in an accidental way, which at that time I had chalked up as an imaginary dream. Where I would have left it, if I had not have had it confirmed to me again, accidentally, many years later.

Our story begins in eastern Canada, in the province of Ontario. I was living on a farm in Muskoka, Ontario. I was not farming at that time. As all of the small mixed farms in that area had been reduced mostly to living quarters, a vegetable garden, and overgrown fields.

This would be year 1971. I was at that time employed by the post office, hauling bulk mail from the main post office, which was in the town of Gravenhurst. I would load up there into my one-ton walk-in van. I would then deliver to six post offices as I headed north on highway #69. My sixth and final post office being Parry Sound.

Always being a morning person, this job never did agree with me very well. As it was six days a week, with my workday beginning at 2 a.m. By seven or eight some mornings I was really tired. My truck was near new and a good runner. Also I was familiar with every hill and curve of my daily route. I found out that I could slip into a state of semiconsciousness, almost to the alpha state, and still be able to pilot my truck in a safe and restful manner. It was while in this state of semiconsciousness, one windy, snowy morning just south of Parry Sound, when I had my first peek into the mysterious subject of reincarnation. The projection of pictures and events that came to me that cold February morning were very clear and realistic. So clear in fact that I can still recall them like it was still that cold and snowy morning, some 29 years later.

It was a very bright and sunny morning, but the wind was gusty and cold. I would judge the season to be September or October. The intermittent strong gusts of wind swirled the dry brown leaves around my mount and I. I was riding a tall and rangy horse, which was a solid roan color, except for three white feet. I was aware that my horse was having a hard time walking as he limped heavily on his left front foot. We were slowly progressing down the main street of a town. Which I, at that time, had no idea of name or place. I looked around at the tall false-fronted buildings, the hitching rails, water troughs, etc. I would judge the time to be between 100 and 150 years ago.

The town seemed deserted. Which I understood was due to the early hour. At the far end of the main street, off to my right and 2 or 3 hundred feet away from the other town buildings, was a low shed. It was constructed mostly of vertical boards, cracked and weathered to a silvery gray color. In front of the shed stood a mountain of a man. He wore a leather shirt with the arms missing. A leather apron was tied around his waist and he stoked a blacksmith's forge with the help of a bellows. The bright morning sun glinted off his thick black head of hair, which hung just above his shoulders. I rode up to him and dismounted. It seemed like no greeting was necessary. This big man simply picked up my reins and said in a deep and easy voice, "I'll fix him up for you, Jim."

As he led the horse towards the shed I turned and walked back to the town buildings and the board sidewalk. I worked the stiffness out of my legs.

My boots made a loud, "thunk, thunk," on the dry board sidewalk. My spurs jangled, I felt good. I was happy and hungry all at the same time. As I passed a plate glass window I caught my reflection. Instead of my usual 5 foot 8, 180-pound frame. I was looking at a taller man, I would say approximately 5 foot 10 and a slender 160 pounds. The appearance was good. The body seemed toned and fit. I was dressed in tight-legged blue denims, a heavy red and black plaid shirt and high-heeled style cowboy boots. The Stetson was in new condition and a light tan color. The familiar six-gun hung from a wide bullet studded belt, low and on the right side. The face was lean and good-looking. Darkly tanned with a medium brown, neatly trimmed beard.

I turned to view down the street. WHAM!!! In a split second I was once more a mail truck driver. My right front wheel had hit a pothole, which had developed due to the frost heaves that were common in that area. I was now wide awake and confused at the feeling of reality that was attached to this event. I pulled over to the shoulder of the road to check my wheel and tire. I could not shake off the feeling of this event happening to me so personally. I was struck with many perplexed feelings about it. And a profound sadness that I had been so suddenly brought back to the present. As it so seemed.

At this time I had no other alternative but to pass it off as an imaginary dream that had seemed so real. I got back in my truck and headed homeward.

Many years passed by in my eventful life. This happening that I have just shared with you would resurface every once in a while. I began to unconcernedly realize that there was more to this event than I had realized or understood at the time. But I took it lightly.

CHAPTER TWO

A REAL GOOD LOOK AT REINCARNATION

It was now 1985 and I found myself living in the state of California. A fugitive from the Canadian justice system at that time. I was in a desert town called Desert Hot Springs, which is a few miles north of Palm Springs. Tourists come from all over the world to soak their aching bones in the natural sulfuric hot springs of this desert town.

Being a brick and block mason by trade, I was working on a sand break block wall fence, which surrounded the property of a rich citizen of Desert Hot Springs. It was high noon. My helper and I decided to go to the bar that was close to us for lunch and a beer. This, without me knowing it, was to be a much bigger event for me than a simple lunch break. The name of this bar, by the way, turned out to be "the Alibi."

We sat down at a large round table next to the window. We could see the people coming and going as we sipped our beer and waited for the daily lunch special to arrive. The place was filling up with noon patrons. We were halfway through our lunch special, which turned out to be chili beans, toast, and hamburger steak with onions. I said to my helper as we got another beer. "TAKE A LOOK AT THIS!" She was coming down the sidewalk towards us. She was undeniably beautiful. I judged her at 5 foot 4 inches and 120 pounds. She was shapely. I have never seen better, ever. The face was tanned and beautifully featured. Dark hair hung over one shoulder in a wraparound braid. The shorts and top were white and scanty. I would guess her age at thirty-two. She entered the Alibi. And as the place was just about now to capacity, she took a small table that was to our right, away from the window.

I looked at her and smiled. She smiled back, said hi, and asked how the lunch special was. I informed her of how tasty it was and invited her to sit with us at the big table. As it offered more room and a better view of the street. She seemed very taken with this offer of friendship and quickly sank into a chair on my left. I soon found out that I was very attracted to her and had a hard time to keep from staring. She ordered the special and joined us with the next beer.

Her name was Maggie and she was from Los Angeles. She was here on a weeks holidays. And she was a hypnosis therapist. Not knowing what a hypnosis therapist was, I felt comfortable about asking her to explain to me. She stated that she was able to help troubled people by finding out their troubles through the powers of hypnosis. During the conversation I had mentioned to her that I could not be hypnotized. As I had tried it in the past to no result. She assured me that she would be able to do this to me. I thought to myself, *You can do whatever you like to me.*

We had now ordered our beer number six. It was two o'clock. I informed my helper that he should finish his beer. Go clean up the job site, and then take the rest of the day off, as it was too hot to work anyway. He agreed. Finished his beer and left with a sly wink of his eye.

I now looked gorgeous Maggie square in the eye. I told her that I was very doubtful that her hypnotic powers would work on me. When others had failed twice. Her beautiful face changed to an easy smile. And she asked what I would want to be hypnotized for in the first place. I informed her that, like the other times, it would just be for the experience of being hypnotized.

She crossed her beautiful legs, and smiled again. She told me it would be a complete waste of time and energy for us both, if we didn't have a reason to do this.

"Isn't there some unanswered question or problem in the back of your mind that you would want brought out?" she asked politely. "Most people do, you know."

I scanned her beautiful person and assured her that I had no pressing problems at all. But there was one thing that had stayed in my mind for many years now. And I have often wondered why. I related to her my scenes from the past that I had experienced when driving the mail truck. She informed me that past lives and reincarnation was a very common subject in her administration of patient treatment.

"So you think that these scenes that I have experienced, could be a past life thing?" I asked her thoughtfully.

"Let's say we finish our beers and go find out," she said gaily, "and by the way, I do like Canadians."

Her suite was large and luxurious. One side, which was all glass, looked out onto the deck and the hot springs. The air conditioning was on and it was beautiful. I thanked her as she handed me a cold Budweiser.

As we sipped our beer, she said matter-of-factly, "We will finish our beer and then I'm putting you under. I'm curious to find out what kind of a character you were."

I was also very curious. There was no swinging pendulums or swing lights to follow. This beautiful lady simply seated me in a plush armchair. Feet on a footstool. She leaned her perfect body near to me. Touched my temples with cool soft fingers. She stated that I was now going into a deep hypnotic trance.

And would see scenes from past lives. And that I was to relate in detail everything that I saw and experienced, in a loud and clear voice. The cool fingers were now going from my temples down my neck to my shoulders and back again. She hummed a beautiful relaxing melody that I was unfamiliar with. The fingers caressed and the melody was enchanting me. All of a sudden she was gone and the cold wind was in my face.

The occasional snowflake struck my face leaving a stinging sensation. This was due to the strong headwind that I was riding straight into, and also the fast pace of my horse. He was a long-legged dappled gray. He was running fast but it seemed effortless for this rangy gelding. He seemed to be in a tireless gait. I compared him to a coyote who can run all day if not hurried by anyone or anything. I looked around at my surroundings. I was quite relaxed as the horse's gait was very easy to move with. We were following a trail rather than a road. There were many horse tracks in the sand below us. It was a well-traveled trail but no other riders were in sight, either behind me or on the trail ahead. The desert around us was made up of rolling sand hills, dotted occasionally by cactus trees of various sizes. Mesquite bushes were sparse here. Large clumps of tumbleweed rolled towards us, driven by the raging wind. The wind had picked up, driving more sand into my face. As we reached the summit of one of the rolling hills I pulled the gray to a stop, to let him catch his second wind. I pulled my neck scarf up around my face to stop the sand from entering my breathing passages.

Daylight was just about gone, I realized, as I looked into the black and angry sky. I urged the willing gray onward. He again settled into his easy lope. It seemed to me that he knew where he was going. Possibly to warmth, hay, water and grain. Two to three miles passed quickly beneath us. The wind and sand was now a screaming enemy. I could see something on my left a couple of hundred feet up the trail. I could not make it out due to the oncoming darkness. It looked like only a dark shadow. We were now abreast of it and I pulled the gray to a stop. He shook his head and snorted loudly. As he wanted to be on his way, and I was being a real pain for stopping him. The object turned out to be a direction sign. I edged the gray closer. It was a post approximately eight inches in diameter and six feet high. The sign was a four-foot piece of two-by-eight, sharpened to an arrow point on the one end. And pointing in the direction that we were traveling. The letters had been burnt into the wood by a heated iron. They were uneven and spelled: "Tombstone Eleven Miles."

I gently nudged the big gray with my heels. He sprang forward like a catapult. He needed no urging. He knew where he was going. An unspoken understanding now passed between man and animal. I let him set his own pace, and let him pick whichever side of the trail that he preferred. He now settled into a more relaxed, faster and smoother gait. I could feel my gaunt stomach knotting into hunger pangs. The trail now seemed to fly away beneath us. The cactus and mesquite seemed a blur, in the now encompassing darkness. The gray never faltered or hesitated. Either his eyes were much better than mine, or he was being guided by some magical instinct that only animals of high intelligence can possess.

We were now topping one of the higher hills. As we started down the other side, the big gray whinnied and seemed to lengthen his stride. Scanning the darkness ahead of us I could make out dimly lighted windows a short distance ahead. I pulled the gray down to a walk. And although he was still in a hurry, he did settle for a fast walk. The gray stopped in front of a weathered board door. A tiny window off to one side sent a weak light through its grimy glass. I dismounted and stretched my legs. When I opened the door it got caught by the wind, and slammed back against the outer wall of the building. The gray walked ahead into the weak light of the livery stable. I forced the door back against the screaming wind. Back to its closed position again. The big gray marched straight ahead and into an empty stall.

As if by curtain call, a short old man came into view, making his way from somewhere in back of the building. He wore a battered hat, bib overalls, and walked with a limp. It was warm in the stable, I rubbed my face with my hands to get out the chill of the wind.

The old man spoke. His voice was strong and clear. "Want him rubbed down too, Jim?" he asked as if by habit.

"Yes, give him the best, Hank," I said.

He started towards the gray and then turned back to me as if by afterthought. He fidgeted with his overalls for a moment and then said in a half whisper, as if he was afraid of being overheard, "Be careful tonight, Jim. Talk to Virginia. She will tell you what it's all about."

"Thanks, Hank." I walked out the small side door and crossed the windswept street, the wind was now a howling monster.

The bat wing door was not visible, as the outer storm door was closed against the howling wind and driving snow, which was blowing in steadily now. I slipped back the huge bolt that was keeping the storm door in place. I opened it only wide enough to let my slim body slide through. I didn't want the wind to catch it, as it would now probably tear it from its hinges. I quickly bolted it behind me. I removed my long winter riding coat and hung it from a peg to the right of the door. It was warm and cheerful in here. The huge bar and gaming room was illuminated by chandeliers equipped with kerosene lamps. Six lamps to a chandelier, twelve chandeliers in all.

"There you are, Jim!" This was Virginia. I would know her voice anywhere. She spoke with a tinkling sound, almost like striking the side of a thin crystal glass with a butter knife.

I turned in the direction of that beautiful tinkling voice. "Hello, Virginia," I said, and smiled in her direction.

She put down the glasses that she had been stacking and came towards me. She was a pretty young woman of average height, and a good all-around body. Topped off with a beautiful head of chestnut hair. Her gown was long, ankle length, it was blue velvet with white trim. Around her tiny waist was a wide white belt. She looked stunning. The kerosene lamps seemingly bringing out the highlights in her beautiful chestnut hair. Her eyes were dark brown glowing coals. She came to where I was standing. Stood up on her tiptoes and gave me a little peck on the lips. Then she said, "Bradley and Gordon were here this afternoon, they had a couple of drinks. And then informed everyone who was here at the time that your days were numbered. And when they left they took the trail south, you did not run into them?"

"No, Virginia. There was no one on the trail today. It was too cold and windy for most, unless they really had to be there."

"I have got to get back to work, be careful," said the tinkling voice.

"Thanks, Virginia, I will," I said.

I crossed the length of the barroom. "Hi, Jim. Hi, Bob. Hi, Ebenezer."

Ebenezer was the town marshal, he was a big man, tall and big. He picked his teeth with a broom straw as he looked down at me. His face was passive, he looked his fifty years today. "Got me worried, Jim," he said, "I don't want any unnecessary shooting around here. Gordon and Bradley are bound to be back, you know."

"Thanks for your concern, Ebenezer, I don't want any shooting either."

"Well, maybe you should head up to Dodge, Jim, at least until this settles down."

"It's too cold to head for Dodge, or any other place,

Ebenezer. And there is only one way to settle things down around here with men like Gordon and Bradley. Especially Bradley, he is the hot head."

"I know, I know," retorted Ebenezer. His big handsome face looked sad, like he had been too long on the peace making job. "Well, just use your head and watch your back, Jim, you know I can't be everywhere at once."

"Don't you be too worried about anything, Marshal," I said. "Go do your rounds, everything will be all right."

The big man put on his long coat and swaggered out of the saloon, into the screaming wind and snow.

I continued my walk to the far end of the barroom. From this vantage point I could observe who entered the front door. Also I had the stairs covered, nobody could go up or down, or come out of the rooms onto the balcony without me seeing them. I ordered whiskey. Oscar the barkeep gave me a worried and sorrowful look as he gave me the whiskey. "What's the matter with you?" I asked with a smile.

He gave me another worried look. "That whiskey is on the house, Jim, watch your back," he said.

All these nervous people were making me nervous. I finished my whiskey and headed upstairs to room #17. I was tired. It had been a long day. I washed and changed into black trousers and a white dress shirt, new black shiny boots, and large silver Spanish spurs. I oiled all of my gun's moving parts, and cleaned and soaped the holster. The action was smooth. I pulled a fast draw in front of the mirror. The holster seemed slick and smooth.

That roasting beef had smelled mighty good when I had come in from the cold air. I was now going to try it on for size. I headed downstairs. The piano man was playing, "The Old Chislom Trail." There was now a good lively crowd in the bar. I crossed to the far end of the room again and took a table next to the wall, so that I had a full view of all exits and entrances.

Miss Tinkling Voice came over and I ordered roast beef and baked potatoes. The beef was excellent, well done, but still moist. I was halfway through my steak when the outer storm door opened slightly. A short figure slid through the opening and limped over to Virginia, spoke to her rapidly, then turned and left the barroom, bolting the door behind him.

Virginia made her way over to my table. A jug of ale in her hand. She put her face close to mine and explained in that beautiful voice. "Gordon and Bradley Roberts are now in the livery stable and see that your horse is in. They sent Hank to tell you to come over to the stable and take it like a man. Hank says that they are both quite drunk, and are saying, if you don't come out they will come over and shoot you down right here in the bar." Before I could answer, she said, "Don't you go, I sent Hank to find Ebenezer."

No sooner had she gone than the door opened and in walked Ebenezer. He looked tired, cold, and old. He walked over to where I sat finishing my steak. "Don't you go to the livery, Jim." He made it more of an order than a request.

"I have no intentions of going anywhere, Ebenezer," I said flatly.

No sooner were the words out of my mouth than the storm door burst wide open. Caught by the wind it whipped back against the outside wall leaving the wide entrance as a channel for the raging wind to enter. There, framed by the door casing and driving wind and snow, stood the Roberts boys. Beady pig eyes searching the room for me.

Gordon spotted me first. He made his way into the center of the room, which had now become deadly silent. All that could be heard was the shuffling of feet, as everybody tried to get back out of the way. Gordon's face was flushed from the cold wind and the booze that he had consumed. He came within twenty feet of where I sat. I could see that his eyes were bloodshot and protruding from their sockets.

Brother Bradley came alongside Gordon. His eyes were also red and puffy, his fat gut hanging over his belt. Bradley, I knew, was the crazy one. I realized that I was going to have to watch them both closely if I was going to survive this attack. So far no one had spoken. Both brothers stood as if in a stupor upon finding me here. Bradley, the crazy one, spoke first. Spittle running down his chin.

"Get on yer feet, ya yella dog, I'm a gonna gun ya down in yer tracks."

Ebenezer's loud voice now boomed into the silence of the room. "Nobody's gunning anybody down in here tonight. Gordon, you take Bradley and get to hell out of here before I lock you both up for causing a disturbance."

Both brothers now turned their dull-witted attention to Ebenezer.

Gordon spoke to Ebenezer. "I'm going to gun this bastard down, Marshal, a fair gun fight is still number one law around these here parts."

Ebenezer now bellowed, loosing his patients, "There will be no gun play in this saloon tonight, that is my law, keep your fair gun fights out in the street or where ever."

"But Marshal," Bradley the stupid one stammered, "it's too dark and windy outside."

At this point I got on my feet and said in a loud and even voice, "You boys meet me out in the street tomorrow at sunup, seven a.m. sharp, and don't be late. Now go get some rest, you will need it."

"All right," said Gordon, in a defeated voice. "Seven a.m. and don't try sneaking out on us through the night." Both men turned and headed for the door, which was still wide open.

Dawn came quickly that day. I dressed in jeans and a heavy, warm doeskin shirt. I checked my side arm and buckled it on. I checked the time on my pocket watch, six-thirty a.m. I slid the gold timepiece back into my pocket, turned and headed downstairs. The barroom was silent and eerie in its emptiness. I looked behind the bar for paper and pen. I found a dip pen and ink along with a large piece of sketch paper. I quickly drew a map showing landmarks and buildings. At a certain spot marked X, I wrote. Gold coins are buried here, $60,000 worth. I folded the map and found an envelope, put the map in and sealed it. I addressed the envelope to Virginia Fleming. Open only if I am killed today, Sunday, December 10, 1852. Signed, James Dillon.

I checked my gold watch again, six-forty. I walked to the window and pulled back the shade enough to look out. The day was clear. The sun was just beginning to peek over the tops of the easterly buildings. The boardwalks on both sides of the street were lined with curious onlookers. Word had got around, the stage, it seemed, was set. I checked Big Ben, one minute to seven. I placed the envelope addressed to Virginia in the mail rack on the office door. I tied down my holster with the leather thongs, pulled up my shirt collar, then pulled back the door bolt and stepped out onto the boardwalk.

The small crowd was silent. No one spoke. But I felt all eyes on me. The early morning air was brisk. But no wind blew. The only evidence of a snowstorm were vivid patches of it here and there, where the wind could not get at it to whip it away. I looked south, the street was empty. I now looked north, two figures were approaching from the far end of town, walking quickly, and abreast, down the center of the street. I stepped off of the boardwalk and into the street. The sandy earth was frozen solid beneath my boots. I could see the Roberts boys more clearly now. They were moving quickly, as if to get there and get it over with. I could now see the vapor from their breathing as it vaporized into the cold air. I felt no fear, only caution. I looked into the sun and took a deep breath. I thought, *Things shouldn't have to be this way.*

The Roberts boys were now approximately thirty feet in front of me. They stopped. They were both bug-eyed and showed fear.

Gordon spoke, his voice was edgy and overly loud. "You're dealing with me now, Dillon." His left hand was posed over his stomach. He was about to execute a cross draw from his holster on his right side, the pistol facing backwards in the holster.

"All right, Gordon," I said, and was somewhat surprised at myself for sensing a slight humor in this pair of clowns, at such an inappropriate time as this. "And what about you, Bradley?" I asked.

The stupid one looked at me, spittle on his mouth and chin as always. He seemed very agitated and nervous. Like he would rather be anywhere, just as long as it wasn't here and now. He haltingly blurted in my direction, "I'm here for backup, Dillon, just in case one of yer friends tries steppin' in." He looked at Gordon as if for assurance that they were on the right track. But Gordon's full attention was now on me and only me. His hand moved slowly, a little closer to that backwards pistol grip. Things now happened very quickly.

"Go for it, Dillon!" shouted Gordon, as his hand darted for the pistol.

Instinctively and for natural want for survival, my right hand dipped for the holster. Before I even knew it, I was fanning the hammer with my left hand, as my second forty-five slug from my pistol entered the big man's chest. When my first slug had hit him, he lurched backwards, his gun hand going up and shooting harmlessly towards the clear blue sky. When slug number two hit him, he lurched backwards once more. He tried to right himself as he looked at me with an expression of surprise and sheer panic. Gordon Roberts then fell face down into the frozen street of Tombstone. Bradley, his dull mind now locked in the survival mode, had drawn and fired at the same instant that Gordon had started his face fall towards the frozen street. I felt the bullet enter my side just below the rib cage. I dropped to one knee as my forty-five spoke again. We had fired almost simultaneously. I felt the burning sensation and the terrible tearing sensation, as the second bullet entered my chest, just below the heart. Bradley had been driven back and was now in a sitting position in the middle of the street. Blood was spreading quickly over the front of his shirt. He stared at me stupidly, as if in disbelief. His eyes blinked like a horny toad as he toppled to his right side and lay still.

I put my hand to my chest. It came away wet and sticky. The pain was minimal. I tried to stand up from my kneeling position. The street, the people, the buildings, all began spinning around as if in a butter churn. I began to feel warm and relaxed, as the darkness slowly surrounded me and engulfed me completely.

"Welcome to Desert Hot Springs," came the pleasant voice of Maggie. "I thought I would have to send the undertaker for you," she joked.

I was slightly confused, I looked slowly around. I was still in the luxurious armchair. My feet were still propped up on the footstool. My hand went instinctively to my chest, the experience had been so real. My hand came away dry. I was all right. I was in California. It was December 10, 1985. Not December 10, 1852. I have often wondered since about the coincidental date of December 10th.

This beautiful woman called Maggie, and I, became inseparable for the next two years of our lives. We did take a trip back to Tombstone via the armchair. I wanted to have another look at that treasure map that I had drawn for Virginia. The lady with the tinkling voice, on December 10, 1852.

With Maggie's expertise help, I was able to sketch a copy of this map while viewing the original, under hypnosis. In that barroom in Tombstone, December 10, 1852.

Maggie and I took off one bright and sunny day in 1986 in my Lincoln convertible. The weather, as I mentioned, was beautiful. We had the top down on the Lincoln and were basking happily in the sunshine as we headed north on I-5 highway. We were heading for the state of Kansas. Dodge City was our destination.

A lot of landmarks, as far as buildings were concerned, had been obliterated due to the passing of time. We were directed now by the remaining landmarks, which were a stream, a huge cottonwood tree, now a huge rotting stump, and a large round boulder laced with white quartz.

This $60.000 in gold coins had been buried by James Dillon, halfway, in a direct line, between this large round boulder and the huge cottonwood tree, which I have mentioned was now a huge rotting stump. We stretched a mason's line from the stump to the boulder. The distance measured out at 114 feet. Using a 100-foot measuring tape we measured along the mason's line to the 57-foot mark. We then marked it with a stake. There seemed to be quite an indenture in the earth, at the location of our stake. I would say approximately one to two inches deeper than the rest of the surrounding terrain, and in a circle of two and one half to three feet. We became very excited. I went to the Lincoln and got the metal detector. I adjusted the setting for the proper land mineral rejection and passed it over the indentured burial spot. Nothing happened. No beep of uncovered gold coins was heard. Virginia, with the tinkling voice, had recovered them those many long years ago. She probably cooled herself under the shade of the huge cottonwood tree while resting from her digging. I was very glad that she had recovered this treasure, as it proved that things had went as planned.

This story will always leave me with many unanswered questions. For example. What really was Virginia to me, James

Dillon? Where had the $60.000 in gold coin come from in the first place? Why were the Roberts boys so set on killing me? Perhaps a lot of these questions of the past are better left in the past. But one can not help but wonder how many other caches of gold coins are still out there, in cases where things did not go as planned?

CHAPTER THREE

LIFE ON THE DESERT

After our return from Dodge City, where we had motored in search of James Dillons' $60,000 in gold coins, Maggie realized that I would never live in Los Angeles. So she had decided to give up her position in the Los Angeles clinic, where she had been employed for many years, and join me in the Coachella Desert. We took up residence in Cathedral City, which is a few short miles southeast of Palm Springs. We rented a three-bedroom bungalow on Elvis Presley Boulevard and settled in. Maggie had many job offers from the surrounding clinics in Palm Springs and Rancho Mirage, as her services were quite in demand. She instead decided to take a long-deserved holiday from her work, and as she quoted it, "Get me on my mysterious and undiscovered road to adventure."

It was now the first week in March 1986. The desert was becoming unbearably hot: 100 to 110 degrees Fahrenheit. I was finishing a ceramic tile contract in Rancho Mirage, at the home of Chuck Connors. Most people will better remember this man

Chuck Connors as the TV series star of the 1960s *The Rifle Man*. Having had the fortunate pleasure of meeting this celebrity on a one-to-one basis. I was deeply and severely awakened to, as I will word it, "The Ravishes of Time." This six-foot-four picturesque hero of the silver screen was now reduced to a white haired, very thin, and very stooped from spinal arthritis old man. Although his eyes were bright and his spirit seemed strong, I nevertheless left him with a profound sadness, as to what the ravishes of time can, and will do, to us all.

I made my way back to Elvis Presley Boulevard to spend some time with Maggie. "God it's hot outside, Maggie," I informed her. As we sat down to a late lunch: cheese and onion sandwich with potato salad, one of my favorites.

"Yes, I am aware of the temperature," said Maggie cheerfully. "That's why I am inside with the air conditioning set at 70 degrees Fahrenheit. I realize how much you appreciate the outdoors," she went on. "So I am inviting you to go with me up to Big Bear Mountain. It is nice and cool up there. And I want you to meet my old Aunt Betsey."

"It would be more than pleasant to feel some cool weather again," I readily assured her. "When did you want to go?"

"We can leave in the morning," she answered.

"Let's do it," I said.

It was only 6 a.m., but fully daylight on the desert. We packed very light for this trip. A couple of overnight bags and a cooler for drinks. We were now in the Lincoln and on our way north. When we left Rancho Mirage on highway #111, a large desert jackrabbit was running with us on our right. They liked to do this. Just for sport, I slowed the Lincoln to match the rabbit's pace. The speedometer on the dash of the Lincoln recorded his top speed at 34 miles per hour. These creatures always held me in wonderment, not only were they great runners, but as I had learned about them, they live to an expected 9 or 10 years of age. And never once do they experience the great pleasure of drinking water or any other liquid. Their sustaining moisture coming strictly through the vegetation that they consume, and also from the atmosphere that they breathe.

CHAPTER FOUR

BIG BEAR MOUNTAIN

We were now north of Palm Springs on highway #62. We were gaining altitude very quickly as we were fast approaching Yucca Valley, which is 1000 feet above sea level. Palm Springs being 2 feet below sea level. At Yucca Valley the country leveled out again, and we cruised past very interesting rock formations on both sides of the two-lane highway. Rock colors ranging from gray, to dark purple, to dull orange. We were now on highway #247 and heading for Lucerne Valley. Where we would make a left hand turn and head southwest on junction #18, which would start us on our steep and long climb, of switchbacks, and hairpin turns, that made up Big Bear Mountain's treacherous east pass.

I would judge this steep climb to be approximately 20 miles, and we were now better than halfway up. I noticed the heat gauge on the Lincoln's dash going up dangerously above the normal reading. Being as we had only 4 cans of Sprite in the cooler, I decided to try to get over the summit without adding the Sprite. As I realized the whole radiator system would then have to be flushed to rid it of the sugar content of the Sprite.

We made the summit. The Lincoln was now throwing a generous cloud of steam from under the hood. As we reached the summit we started immediately downhill on the other side. I shut the engine off and let her coast, which we did for approximately two miles. When the ground leveled off we coasted to a stop beside a large and almost dry lake. As I was to learn after, there had been two lakes in the beginning: Big Bear Lake and Little Bear Lake. Little Bear Lake being at a higher altitude than Big Bear Lake, had been channeled and drained into Big Bear Lake, which had been dammed at the west end, and thus creating one large Big Bear Lake. This large lake had attracted the millionaires from Los Angeles to use as a retreat from their certain stress. Of life in the fast lane in crime city L.A.

The only water left in this Little Bear Lake was away out in the middle of this desert-like lake bed. About a mile from where we were parked. However, about 200 yards away I could see a small jet of water spurting out of the lake bed. It spurted approximately 5 feet in the air and then arched back to the sand. This was an artisan water vein, which had supplied the water to form this lake, before the interference of man. I emptied out the cooler and headed for the water jet. I ran a couple of gallons into the cooler and fed it to the Lincoln. The engine cooled down fine, and we were once again knights of the road.

Big Bear City itself turned out to be a beautiful land of ponderosa pines and green grass, which stretched in an approximate 15-mile strip of houses, hobby farms, roadhouses, saloons, resorts, restaurants, and general stores.

Aunt Betsey, whom I met immediately upon arrival, was a frail 78 years of age, and like her niece, I could see she had been a beauty. I found her bright, interesting, and pleasant. She had lived in Big Bear all of her life. She related to me that she had actually witnessed, in her very early years, to-the-death gun duels that had erupted in and around the settlement of Big Bear.

Mostly, she informed me, they were due to disputes over the many gold claims that were then active at Big Bear Mountain. It was still early afternoon and I was just literally basking in the cool mountain air, which I would judge to be around 65 degrees Fahrenheit. I informed Maggie that she could visit with Aunt Betsey and I would take a look around.

"Okay," was her reply, "we will eat at six."

"Okay," I told her, and left.

CHAPTER FIVE

THE CRAZY HORSE SALOON

I put the top down on the Lincoln and cruised the strip, which seemed real busy for a Tuesday. I was guided by the "Unseen Forces," into a parking lot that put me smack in front of the "Crazy Horse Saloon." When I say I was guided by the unseen forces, I am very serious. As I have noticed throughout my life that I have somehow been guided by these forces, into most of my life's situations, rather than by planned activity. And even in cases of planned activity, it seems that these forces can easily have you sidetracked, as to bring about your plan as it was meant to be in the first place.

I can compare this situation somewhat to an animal that follows a game trail through the dense forest. This game trail will zigzag and double back on itself. But the animal will still follow it, as he is being guided, I have learned, by the veins of magnetic force that run every which way beneath the surface of the earth. We cannot feel them, but the animal can, through its instinctive reaction to these things that are mostly unknown to humans. While we sit and judge ourselves to be the superior intelligence of the universe.

The old men on the bench in front of the saloon were eyeing my Lincoln convertible. And seemed to be reminiscing amongst themselves of a day long ago, which had been much brighter and more promising than today.

I gave them a "Good morning, gentlemen," as I passed, and was rewarded with tobacco juice being spat to the earth at their feet, and toothless grins.

I entered the Crazy Horse Saloon. The door was wide open. The place was empty except for one customer and one bartender. I took a seat at the bar close to these fellows. The bartender was a long slim six foot two, dressed in cowboy attire, including the Stetson hat. He was 55 going on 25. I found out his name was Guy. I introduced myself.

"So you came all the way down from Canada to see us, aye?" he asked.

"Yes," I told him. "Is my accent that noticeable?" I asked.

"Yes, to me it is," he said with a grin.

"Good," I said, and ginned back at him. We hit it off right from the start and became friends that day. The only other customer, who was sipping beer on my right, was introduced to me by Guy the bartender. His name was Donnie Morningstar. He was approximately 35 years of age, average size and build. I learned he was a half-breed Apache, who was employed in the area by the rich locals, as a professional horse breaker. We were now on our fourth beer and having a good old time. Four young women came in and were very happy and sociable. Donnie Morningstar got up and informed us that he was on his way.

"You're welcome to another cold one with us," I informed him.

"Yes, I know," he replied, "but I'm afraid of the creature." Not knowing what he was referring to as, "the creature," I bade him a hearty goodbye. He left abruptly. The four girls finished their drinks and left. We were now down to just Guy and myself in the barroom.

"Well," said Guy, "let's enjoy the peace and quiet, as the evening crowd will soon be here, they start coming in shortly after six and then all hell breaks loose."

Out of curiosity I asked Guy, "What did Donnie Morningstar mean when he left and stated that he was afraid of the creature? Do you have a creature of some kind that comes in here with the evening crowd?"

"No, no," laughed Guy, "the creature is somewhere in Morningstar's head." He looked at my puzzled expression and continued. "I'll set the record straight for you, Terry, I'm sure it will even make Donnie and you better friends.

"It was approximately 11 or 12 years ago. There was a real fall down drinking party going on in the west end of town. Apparently some guy's wife had died and he was drowning his sorrows. The party had apparently gone on for several days and nights. Morningstar had joined the festivities some time during the progression of this drunken predicament.

"Someone had picked a fight with Donnie. And during the ruckus that followed, Morningstar beat this guy senseless on the kitchen floor. He had then retrieved a butcher knife from the cupboard, and then he actually scalped the poor guy. He was charged, and proven guilty, by several eyewitnesses who were present at the party. Morningstar was sentenced to 10 years in Walla Walla. He served his full time, and has only been out for the last couple of years or so. He's had lots of time to think about it. And he truly believes that there is another spirit inside of him. That is all Apache, and prejudice to the point of total destruction to the white man. This is what he refers to as the creature, and why he is afraid to have more than four drinks at one time. As he states, 'He doesn't want to wake the creature.'"

"Thanks for the information, Guy," I told him, "that is really quite a story that you just related to me."

"It is," Guy agreed.

"I must be on my way," I told him, "my ladies are serving dinner at six."

Dinner at Aunt Betsy's was an assortment of delicious and attractively prepared cold cuts, which we topped off with a two liter bottle of California white wine. I, knowing Maggie's inquisitive nature so well, told her and Aunt Betsey of my afternoons adventure in the Crazy Horse Saloon.

Aunt Betsey's first reaction was one of surprise that I had actually, and so quickly, become so familiar with the Crazy Horse. Her next reaction was words of warning: as it being a good idea to stay away from this notorious place, and also from the people that frequented it. She concluded with, "Everything negative in Big Bear happens in the Crazy Horse, Terry."

I assured Aunt Betsey that I had not planned to make the Crazy Horse a hangout for me when visiting Big Bear. I now related to the eager to listen Maggie the strange and tragic story connected to Donnie Morningstar.

Unsurprisingly, she stated, "I would like to meet Mr. Morningstar."

I also wanted her to meet Mr. Morningstar and see if she could make some connection with "the creature."

"Well, let's you and I go down tomorrow afternoon, Maggie, and see if we can run into Mr. Morningstar," I suggested.

"Sounds like an exciting idea," answered Maggie.

"Want to come, Aunt Betsey?" I asked.

"Not on your life," was her firm and final answer.

We stayed in that night. I rented a movie to watch with Aunt Betsey. It was an old favorite of mine from the 1950s. It was entitled, *Thunder Road*. Starring Robert Mitchum in his prime, as a Kentucky moonshine runner. We all enjoyed this stroll down old memory lane. And retired to our snug beds with visions of fast cars, and the beautiful sound of open dual exhaust pipes, roaring in our ears of yesteryear.

Aunt Betsey was an early riser. I could hear the dampers and doors of that old wood cookstove banging and clanging. And as I was now to learn, Aunt Betsey always prepared the breakfast meal on this beautiful old wood cookstove, winter and summer.

"As the wood fire," she explained, "chased the cool and damp night air out of this rambling old house." The house being very large and constructed from ponderosa pine logs, 8 to 10 inches in diameter. I checked my watch, 6 a.m. right on the button.

"Morning, Maggie."

"Morning, yourself," was her reply. I was about to get out of bed and start my day, but Maggie had other ideas that were not hard to accommodate at all.

It was now 7 a.m., as I passed through the huge kitchen on my way to the bathroom. The rich and pleasing aroma of sugar cured bacon and fried eggs hit me smack in the face. I could see them sizzling and snapping in the two large cast iron frying pans on top of that dear old wood cookstove, which was interestingly constructed of black iron, cast iron, and very much chrome platting.

"Morning, Aunt Betsey. Things sure smell good around here," I informed her as I headed for the lavatory. As I quickly showered and shaved, I first mused at myself. But ended up not musing, but marveling at my good fortune. Let's face it, here I was, a middle-aged fugitive from the Canadian justice system. A dirt farm boy with grade school education. And I had just been loved by one of the most beautiful Californian girls that I had ever laid eyes on. And my breakfast, which promised to be the most scrumptious on earth, was being prepared for me by one of our true pioneers, and on a beautiful old wood cookstove. And the sun was rising with the promise of a gorgeous day to come. Behind the locked door of that bathroom that morning, I got humbly down on my knees, and I did thank my "Great Creator of Forces," for the many, many blessings that had been so miraculously bestowed upon me.

We had now retired to Auntie's large front veranda, which, by the way, continued around the entire perimeter of the house. Sugar cured bacon and farm fresh eggs with bright orange yolks were now digesting in our stomachs. I felt over deservedly good. We were all very happy that bright and sunny morning on top of Big Bear Mountain.

"Do you realize what I didn't do, Maggie?" I asked her, as I gazed down at my high-topped dress boots. "I forgot to bring my running shoes with us. So instead of running this morning, let's say we take a walk across to the other side of the highway. Then we can jump into Big Bear Lake and swim out to that island that looks to be about a quarter of a mile away."

"I'm game," replied Maggie.

Aunt Betsey looked at us in disbelief. "Don't you two realize that it is only March 10th? The ice has only been out of the lake for a month, you will die from exposure."

"Okay, Aunt Betsey," said Maggie, "we will go over and test the water first."

This we did and we found the water exceedingly cold. But both of us seemingly needing a challenge that gorgeous morning, we jumped in and made the island in about 20 minutes. One thing about swimming in cold water, the air sure seems warm and relaxing when you come out. The island was small and mostly rock. There was really nothing to explore, so we settled to lounge on the sunniest side and improve on our already dark suntans.

The early spring sun was so full of comfort rays that we both dropped off into a deep slumber. Maggie was shaking me. "Wake up, Terry, we should get back. Auntie will probably have lunch ready, she is very punctual with her meal times, and she does hate stragglers."

"Okay," I said, "let's keep Auntie happy, after all she is a great hostess."

Our timing was right on. It was 11:25 when we reached Aunt Betsy's rambling old home. "I thought I would have to call search and rescue for you two," she joked. "But when I saw that you had reached the island I knew everything was under control."

CHAPTER SIX

MAGGIE MEETS MR. MORNINGSTAR

Three-fifteen p.m. found the gorgeous Maggie and I sitting in the Crazy Horse Saloon sipping a cold Budweiser. Guy, the bartender and owner, was much overdoing it in his quest to get Maggie's attention. He had already wiped our table three times, and overcrowded us with complimentary peanuts. It was customary in the Crazy Horse to shell your peanuts and dispose of your shells on the floor. This custom, which was the custom of all the roadhouses in Big Bear, always struck me as a very high fire hazard. But much to my surprise, I never did hear of fire breaking out due to this custom.

"Has Donnie Morningstar been around today?" I asked Guy.

"Not yet," said Guy, "he usually makes it in around four." More customers were coming in and Guy left us to serve them. We were halfway through our first beer when I noticed Donnie Morningstar come in. He headed for the bar to speak with Guy. Guy being busy with the quickly increasing number of customers, directed Donnie over to our table. "Hi," said Donnie cheerfully. "Guy said that you were asking about me so I thought I would come over and say hi."

"I'm glad you did, Donnie," I answered him assuredly. "And this is my main lady, Maggie." They shook hands, with Morningstar eyeing her approvingly. When the pleasantries were over with, I said, "Donnie, I hope you don't take offence, or even feel uncomfortable about what I am about to tell you. And I make this statement due to the very short time that we have known each other. What I am referring to is what you call, 'the creature.' You see, Guy and I got talking after you left yesterday, and he related the whole story of your misfortune to me. And as Guy put it, he thought it would make you and I better friends."

Mr. Morningstar looked at us with slight amusement, and assured us that it was perfectly all right that we were now aware of his past. One reason being, the old Apache belief was that the more people that were involved in sharing your burden the easier it then became for the burdened one to carry it. And his personal feelings were regulated to where he was not, in the least, ashamed of his past. Just a wiser and more cautious man for the happening of it all.

I now felt comfortable about proceeding with our side of the story. And so I quickly related to Donnie what Maggie done for a living. I also told him a bit about the adventures that she had taken me on, via the armchair. "We were thinking that possibly through the power of hypnosis that you may be able to contact the creature, and possibly, reach some kind of truce towards peace of mind."

Mr. Morningstar mulled this one over real well, as a matter of fact, he mulled it over two more Budweisers. As I ordered the next round I realized that was Donnie's fourth and final drink of the day. The poor guy grudgingly told us that he would probably, down deep, like to do this. But he was just too afraid of awakening the creature to proceed with it.

"Well," said Maggie, "the only way that we would even consider doing this is when you feel 100 percent sure that you want to proceed with it." Maggie gave him our phone number in Cathedral City and informed him to think it over real well, and to call us anytime with any questions that may arise in the future. And also that we definitely would be back periodically, to visit with Aunt Betsey, and would look forward to seeing him on those occasions. This seemed to sit very well with Mr. Morningstar and he left the barroom abruptly and happily.

"He will want to do this soon, I think," I stated to Maggie.

"I was just thinking the same thing," said Maggie cheerfully. "I do hope so as I am really looking forward to meeting the creature."

"And so was I," I laughingly assured her. We finished our beer and informed Guy that we would be seeing him again in the real near future.

We decided to spend a quiet evening with Auntie again, as we had to be heading back to Cathedral City in the morning. Our video that night was *North to Alaska*, starring big John Wayne, Stewart Granger, and Fabian.

Aunt Betsey enjoyed it immensely, and believe it or not, she was seeing it for the first time. She was still talking about it at breakfast the next morning, she had so thoroughly enjoyed it. Also she did comment to the fact that she did enjoy John Wayne's performance. But much preferred Robert Mitchum as her personal choice of an actor model.

I assured her that next time it would be Robert Mitchum, and Robert Mitchum only, as far as movies went.

Our trip down the treacherous east side pass of Big Bear Mountain was smooth and enjoyable. We started to feel the desert heat again as we cruised through Lucerne Valley. Yucca Valley was a few degrees hotter.

By the time we reached Desert Hot Springs, the thermometer was hitting 110 degrees Fahrenheit. We made a beeline for

Cathedral City and our air-conditioned bungalow on Elvis Presley Boulevard.

Maggie and I sat down to a late lunch consisting of cottage cheese, sliced tomatoes, and sliced cucumbers dipped in vinegar, great hot weather food.

"Do you have any idea what I am thinking right now, Maggie?" I asked her. "And have been thinking for the past two hours."

"Not really," said the beautiful Maggie with a questioning look. "But I wouldn't mind betting that it's got something to do with the heat, which I realize is just not your type of weather."

"Let me explain myself," I answered patiently. "I am not the type of a guy who will sit and bitch about the situation." I learned a long time ago that you either accept the situation for what it is, or you do something about it, in the direction of making it more acceptable, or by changing it completely. And with the situation at hand, it is going to be the latter. Change it completely. "Maggie dear, I'm moving up to Big Bear Mountain, what do you want to do?"

"I'm with you," was her immediate answer. "I do plan to take the rest of this year off. So I don't have to be in any particular place at any particular time."

CHAPTER SEVEN

RETURN TO BIG BEAR

April the first was our planned day for moving out of, "The Frying Pan," as I had so meaningfully nicknamed the Coachella Desert during the summer months, which took in 8 months of our calendar 12. The only time that the desert made perfect sense to me were the months of November, December, January, and February.

This was the snowbird season. The migration of all the retirees and other travelers to migrate to a perfect winter Shangri-la. The temperature would hold steady through these months at from 65 to 80 degrees Fahrenheit. The perfect sunny skies being an every day expectancy. Broken only by one or two days of wind, and possible rain, throughout this entire four-month period. But take my experienced word for it, by March first, be packed and be on your way north, as this is the time Mother Nature brings out, "The Frying Pan." I hope that you readers don't get the idea that I am shunning the desert. This is much to the contrary, as I have studied this enchanting land. And have found countless subjects that were of extreme interest to my inquisitive nature. A few of these I want to share with you. And will do so by infiltrating them throughout this story.

Now if you happen to be a snowbird. Do stay on the desert for the month of February. As this is spring on the desert. Nowhere in the world will you experience a more beautiful and interesting array of wildflowers and tree blossoms. You will marvel at the usually drab sand dunes being completely strewn with nature's arrangements of acres of bright red and orange devils paint brushes. Hillsides ablaze with beautiful yellow shades of buttercups, and countless other species and colors of Mother Nature's arrangement.

Telling us in whispers of pink and mauve, "Spring is here."

Being as we realized that accommodations for rent were next to impossible in Big Bear City, and especially at this time of the season, we quickly decided to take the motor home up the mountain. This motor home was an older model, but very livable and comfortable. I had bought it up in Muskoka, Canada. And had traveled down here to California with it serving as both my transportation and my home away from home. It was a 24-foot South Wind on a Dodge chassis. Powered by a 440 Chrysler engine. The only complaint that I had about this unit was the fact that some previous owner had changed the fuel from gasoline over to propane. Now this made perfect sense in Canada in 1985, as propane at that time was only half the price of gasoline. However in California, prices were about equal, and service centers were few and far between. Resulting in making sure that your second tank was always completely shut off, and used for emergency purposes only. Now anyone who has driven a heavy vehicle fired by propane, will readily agree with me to the fact that compared to gasoline, 30 percent of your combustible power has been lost with this alternative fuel.

And being as this motor home weighed exactly six tons, without us and our belongings, I can assure you that I have had some breath holding, and also embarrassing moments, while piloting this old baby. Most of these moments we will get to a little later on in the story. But there is one that did strike my sense of humor at the time, which I would like to share with you now.

Most of you will recall this old song that has been around for ages, "Hotrod Lincoln." Well, there is a certain line in that song that goes like this:

"We were driving up Grapevine Hill passing cars like they were standing still."

This song was going through my mind one night while I was in fact climbing this same Grapevine Hill that they refer to in the song.

On my way out of San Pedro. This Grapevine Hill is twisty and very, very, steep. Now I want you to picture that motor home of mine. Far over on the outside lane and moving at a snail's pace, the tractor-trailers were passing me effortlessly. I was very concerned as my transmission was automatic and I knew if she stalled that the park gear wouldn't hold her on a steep hill. And I doubted that the brakes would hold her either, if she did stall. But it never did, "touch wood."

This propane fired unit was about to be tested again as to its hill climbing ability. It was April the first. Maggie and I were packed. We boarded our Southwind Home away from home, and were Big Bear bound. It was 6 a.m. as we left Cathedral City. We had decided to climb some altitude before the heat of the day hit us. Seven-thirty found us pulling into Lucerne Valley on highway #247. In a few minutes we would be at junction #18 and the beginning of our climb, up the treacherous east pass of Big Bear Mountain. I pulled into a service center to check out the cooling system. The radiator was topped up and I replaced a couple of belts that didn't look that substantial. We were now fueled up and on our way.

"There's one thing concerning me, Maggie," I said.

"Could that be that you are already missing the frying pan?" she teased me laughingly.

"Good joke, Maggie, but no that's not it," I told her, "it's much more serious than that." I then related to her the story of Grapevine Hill, and the steep climb that we had in front of us right now. "I don't mean to make you nervous and spoil your trip, Maggie, but I have got to have you prepared. You see this motor home has an automatic transmission. Now if it stalls on the hill, the park gear won't hold much. Also I'm sure that the brakes won't hold it either on a real steep incline. As they don't work near as good going backwards. And this old baby weighs exactly six tons. Also you see that I have no side door on my side. The right side has the only entrance or exit door. Now if I holler, jump. Do it fast, as we will both be jumping out of that same door."

She gave me a real serious look and repeated my words. "Yes, if you holler jump, let's do it fast."

I smiled at her reassuringly and headed up the pass. Things were progressing better than I had expected, and we were now approximately halfway up the pass. But we were definitely moving slow. I was now leading quite a procession. At the last switchback I was able to hurriedly count 13 vehicles of all shapes and sizes. Hot on our tail. Where they would be staying until we got over the summit. As there were no traffic turnouts on this road. Just two lanes carved into the mountainside.

The heat gauge was staying at a steady three quarter needle point. We were now on the final half-mile to the summit and the steepest part of all. Maggie had recently informed me that we now had 20 followers. She took a quick look ahead. Unlatched the side door and sat on the edge of her seat, all eyes. Like I say, we were slow. But that damned propane just wouldn't quit. We crept over the summit at a slow walk. Where I immediately pulled off to the right to let our, now frustrated, followers get on their way.

You could have bought me for a nickel as this procession passed us. We experienced everything from stern dirty looks, to poisoned messages. All thrown in the direction of my side window. I pretended that I could not hear, or see. I gave Maggie a big wide grin and she quickly rewarded me with the sweetest kiss that I have ever experienced. "Quite a hot rod Lincoln," she jeered through her laughter.

We let the dust settle. Thanked the "Great Creator" for our many blessings and were on our way to Aunt Betsy's. All arrangements had been made with Auntie. We were going to park the motor home on her back acreage. From there we could cut into her water line, and also the sewer line. I had purchased 200 feet of weatherproof electrical cable that would easily reach from the fuse box in the log house out to the motor home. Aunt Betsey was overjoyed to have us around for a while. And everyone had agreed to it being a better idea with the motor home, as to the other alternative of living with Auntie. As this way no one was being forced to give up their privacy.

CHAPTER EIGHT

FAT BILLY COMES TOO BIG BEAR

A personal friend of mine Bill Mcphee, to whom I had given the nickname of "Fat Billy the Roofer," was bringing the Lincoln up to Big Bear for us.

He had heard me talking about the Crazy Horse Saloon, and about the characters that hung out there. He had suggested that he would bring the Lincoln up for me on Saturday morning, stay over, and then take a bus back to Desert Hot Springs on Sunday. This way he could get away from Desert Hot Springs for a while. As well as to get to spend an evening at the Crazy Horse Saloon. Billy was always afraid that he might be missing something. Also he loved driving my Lincoln convertible. And couldn't keep his eyes off of Maggie. Adding all of this together, I was more than positive that Fat Billy the Roofer would be there as planned. And he was.

Let me tell you a bit about this character, "Fat Billy the Roofer," as a kind of introduction. Bill Mcphee was in his late thirties. He was a 5 foot 6 inches, much overweight Irishman. American born. He had been born, and grew up in the state of Pennsylvania. Pittsburgh being his hometown. Billy and his brother Ron had drifted down to the California desert area in the mid seventies. When the steel mills of Pennsylvania were in a state of recession.

They had drifted around California for a year or two. Living in Los Angeles, Orange County, Whittier, and Bill finally settled in the Desert Hot Springs area. He had married a little Mexican woman, and were by 1985, when I first met Bill, working on their sixth child. Fat Billy the Roofer was at this time posing as a roofing contractor. He had a battered Ford pickup with a ladder mounted on the top, and a few shingles and hand tools in the box.

Now Billy, in spite of being overweight, had a good appearance. He had a very healthy complexion, under a thick blond head of curly hair. Mr. Mcphee's greatest gift, to my estimation, was the great gift of the silver tongue. I have never seen him bettered in a verbal argument or discussion of any kind. This man was educated as well as gifted. When he lit you up with that genuine smile of his and started to talk, you were just automatically listening to each and every word that flowed fluently from this Irish devil's mouth. His main income at this time was derived from down payments on roofing contracts. He would run ads and fliers in the Palm Springs and Rancho Mirage area newsprints for roofing and reroofing contracts. Upon getting a call for his services he would put on a clean shirt and head out in the old truck in the direction of his next victim.

Now this desert area was just plum full of rich, and very rich citizens of all ages. Fat Billy was in a financial paradise. When reaching his destination it was only a matter of minutes that it would take Billy to have their confidence completely. And would have them assured of how expertly he would be able to solve their roofing problem. Then out would come the contract sheet. So much in advance to cover the material cost. And the remainder to be paid on job completion. Which, to my knowledge, Fat Billy had never experienced a job completion. Even I, in the beginning, wondered just how this rascal was getting away with this deception, which he exercised so brashly and openly. Fat Billy never gave the least sign of any fear of reprimand in this direction. As he explained to me a thousand or two dollars didn't really mean a lot to most of these people. Also his area of operation was large, you just have to be careful not to get two houses in a row on the same street, he stated with his genuine grin now in place. And you have to call the telephone company every week and have your number changed. Due to all of the obscene phone calls that you are receiving, he told me as his smile widened.

To sum it all up, Fat Billy the Roofer was a con man. One of the smoothest that I have ever met in all of my extensive travels. We did have many laughs and situations together that I will relate to you as our story progresses.

It was Saturday morning. Maggie and I were having a late breakfast under the shade of the canopy that I had erected. I had fastened a heavy tarp to the roof of the motor home and extended it out 16 feet. And running the full 24-foot length of the motor home. It served us very well for a front porch, where we were to spend most of our summer. We went to a couple of local secondhand stores. We purchased some old and cheaply priced, but interesting furnishings for under our canopy, complete with armchairs. We were comfortable, we were free and happy. It was summer in Big Bear, 1987.

My cell phone rang. "I know who that is," stated Maggie.

"Well, okay, before I answer, who?"

"I would sat Fat Billy," she answered, a hint of amusement in her eyes.

In spite of her complete knowledge as to Fat Billy's questionable character, I could see that she did like this guy for the rascal that he not only portrayed, but truly was to the core.

And I also felt the same way towards Billy.

"Hello, Bill," I said, taking the chance that it was the rascal.

"Hello, yourself," boomed the fat man. "How did you know it was me? I suppose that you got yourself one of those ten thousand dollar phones where you can see who is on the other end, is that it?" asked Billy jokingly.

"No I'm talking to you from my cell phone, Maggie just seemed to know that it was you. But that telephone with the picture on the other end. Did you ever see one, Billy?" I asked.

"No," he admitted, "just heard about them, I wouldn't be able to afford one anyway."

"Well, I think that maybe you should look into it, and maybe get one on the installment plan," I told him.

"Why is that?" asked Fat Billy.

"Well, I think it would be just the thing for you, Billy. Because you must realize, the same as I do that the California telephone companies are definitely going to run short of numbers sooner or later. And you won't be able to change it every week. This way all you would have to do is just have a good memory for faces."

"Oh, now I see what you are getting at," retorted Billy, laughing, "if I didn't think that was so damned funny, I might be highly insulted. But listen, Ter, Fat-Billy-never-stuck-for-an-answer said, I have a far better idea. If Maggie is so damned good at knowing who is telephoning who. Why don't I just buy her from you and forget about the damned TV telephone entirely." The fat man was laughing hilariously now.

"Well, Billy," I said, "there is nothing wrong with the idea. But since you don't have the price even for the telephone, I think that chances of it working are pretty remote." We were both laughing now.

"Okay, Ter," shouted Billy, "give me directions to your camp, this telephone booth is too small for me."

Billy was under the canopy and stretched out in the biggest, and softest armchair within 10 minutes of our telephone conversation. Maggie, always sociable and happy, went into the motor home and came back with ice-cold Budweisers for us.

"Oh, that reminds me," said Fat Billy. He went over to the Lincoln that he had surprisingly washed and polished to a high luster. He opened the trunk and pulled out a cooler full of beer and ice. "No sense in letting the ice melt in this," he stated, and placed the cooler on the ground between us. I could now see where this day was heading.

"I'm going to put on some CDs," said Maggie. "What do you boys want? You have three choices, which are Dean Martin, Elvis Presley, or Johnny Cash." We agreed on Dean Martin, who came on with, "Send Me the Pillow That You Dream On." We then clinked glasses and toasted Big Bear Mountain.

"It don't get much better," I stated, "we all have good company, the beer is ice cold, and we are being serenaded by one of America's legends."

"And the sun is shining, and the day is still new, and we are all healthy," stated Billy.

"Yes," said Maggie, "I think that we all had better count our blessings. I don't know when I have ever been this happy."

My telephone rang again, interrupting Dean Martin, who was now onto, "Everybody Loves Somebody Somewhere." This time it was Guy calling from the Crazy Horse. "You guys coming over today?" he asked. "I can slip away and pick you up before it gets too busy around here," he offered.

"No, Guy," I answered, "I do appreciate the offer but my friend is here with my Lincoln, so we can drive over and see you. I do want you to meet my friend Billy also, so we'll probably see you within the hour."

"Okay," said Guy, "sounds good, Morningstar is here too and has asked about you and Maggie."

"Okay, Guy," I said, "tell Donnie to wait and have a beer

with us, bye."

"You drive, Billy," I said and we took off down the strip in the direction of the Crazy Horse Saloon. Billy had his arm out the window and his head right back, with a grin that would melt the collar off a priest.

"Next parking lot on your left, Billy," I said. We got a parking slot right next to the front door. Merle Haggard was on the jukebox, serenading the crowd with, "Momma Tried," which was easy to listen to. Guy waved us over to the bar, we said our hellos and I introduced him to Billy.

"I got to keep things moving here," Guy stated. "Morningstar is over there by the jukebox and is saving an entire table for you guys," he said. "Go sit down and I will get you your drinks pronto."

We sat down with Donnie, Fat Billy eyeing him cautiously as if his own scalp was in jeopardy. And I do confess the thought went through my mind momentarily that the thick curly head of hair of Billy's would make one dandy Apache scalp if there ever was one.

Morningstar seemed overjoyed to see us today. At first I thought that maybe he had overrun his four drinks, but I was soon to learn that this wasn't the case. As Guy set down the cold beers, he remarked to Morningstar, "That's your third, Donnie, just in case your not keeping count today."

"I know, I know," said Donnie. "Don't you worry, Guy, I'm more afraid of the creature than what you are." He grinned. "And while we are mentioning the creature," he turned to Maggie, "you know what, pretty lady? I have decided to have a look at the creature, that is if you will do this for me, and think it will work."

"Well," smiled beautiful Maggie, "I would be happy to give it a try for you, and we will hope for good results, okay?"

"Okay," agreed Morningstar. "But when, Maggie? You know now that I have decided, I feel like I can hardly wait."

Maggie turned to Billy and I. "Well, comrades," she said, "are we game to take Mr. Morningstar back to the motor home and see if we can put him in touch with the creature?"

"Sounds like a great idea, Maggie," I said with enthusiasm. "What about you, Billy?" As I asked him I already knew that he wouldn't miss this for anything. "Do you want to stay and enjoy the Crazy Horse for a while or do you want to come?"

"Try to get away without me," was his immediate reply.

We headed for the door. Guy rushed over and asked, "Where you guys going so early?" I quickly related to him about what was to come down. I could tell by Guy's expression just how important this prevalent act that was about to be executed by the gorgeous Maggie was to him, and probably everyone in Big Bear, who was acquainted with Donnie. Or even just his tragic life story.

"Call me just as soon as you know something," was his impatient reply.

"You will be the first, Guy," I assured him. We left with Billy at the wheel. Morningstar's pickup was hot on our tail, and stayed close, like we might disappear on him.

CHAPTER NINE

THE LEGEND OF DONNIE MORNINGSTAR

Mr. Morningstar was now seated under the canopy in the plush old armchair. His feet were up on the footstool. Maggie set up her tape recorder, asked for complete silence from Billy and I, and then began to work her magic.

"You will go into a deep, deep, trance, Donnie," she said in her light and pleasant voice. "You will see and hear things from your past lives, you must relate to me in a clear and loud voice, everything that you see and hear."

Billy and I watched as Morningstar went under. We first noticed that his facial expression had changed, and even though his eyes were closed, his face seemed to take on an expression of extreme cruelty. His fists clenched. His feet and legs twitched. Maggie was looking at him with an expression of complete surprise. Then Donnie's lips seemed to curl up into a cruel grin, and he began to speak. The words came out so abruptly, and so loud that I noticed Maggie, always so composed, draw back to an arm's length from her patient.

The words were coming fast and furious now. The sentences were broken intermittently with loud shrieks, and loud hoots, and hollers. We couldn't understand a word that was coming from this seemingly tortured soul, as he hollered and squirmed in the armchair. Everything was uttered in a language completely foreign to the three of us, which we were soon to learn, was in fact, the original tongue of the Apache Nation. Morningstar began to thrash more violently. His face was contorted into one bad looking dude. His shrieking became almost deafening. I was just about to ask Maggie if she thought she should bring him out, when he suddenly became quiet. His body relaxed. The once so badly contorted face, once more belonged to Mr. Morningstar.

Maggie touched him gently on the temples. "Welcome back to Big Bear Mountain," she said, smiling at him.

Donnie looked confused for a moment, but quickly regained his composure. Grinning at us, he asked with great expectations, "What happened? What did I say?"

"We don't know what you said," stated Maggie. "You spoke everything in a language that we are unfamiliar with. Maybe you will be able to translate for us."

"Sure," said Donnie impatiently, "let's give it a try."

Maggie clicked the recorder over to playback. Morningstar's performance began its eerie message.

"Apache!!!" uttered Donnie in astonishment, as he listened to his playback. I noticed his blank expression and pale complexion. He sat as if transfixed. When the words and shouting became louder, he shrieked, "Shut it off!! Shut it off!!"

Maggie reached over and clicked the machine off, there was now complete silence. Donnie looked around at us as if seeing us for the first time. And not trusting us one inch.

"You okay, Donnie?" I asked.

He didn't answer, instead he looked at Maggie and said flatly, "I want the tape."

Maggie clicked open the recorder, rejected the mystery tape

and handed it to him. "There you are, Donnie," she said.

Donnie didn't speak again. Instead, he made a quick and unsteady beeline for his Chevy pickup and left us with a squeal of tires. And all of us with a profound dumb expression on our faces. We looked at each other for a moment. I spoke first. "Well, Billy, I never thought that I would see the day that you would be stuck for words."

This seemed to break the spell of the mysterious unknown. We all began to relax and laugh. Not because Donnie's situation was a fun thing, but because we didn't know what else to do. And that's really all we could do at that moment.

"You know," confessed Fat Billy, "I have never before in my life experienced a feeling like the one that came over me when Donnie started to squirm and yell. And then even worse when he started to listen to the playback. It was a feeling like I had just stepped into some forbidden place. Or maybe even hell. I just don't know, it really was strange, it was weird," explained Billy. His eyes protruding from their sockets.

"Yes, I know," I said, "I felt just about the same way as you did. What do you make of it, Maggie?"

Maggie's beautiful face wore an expression of deep concern, and her usually perfect composure seemed slightly shaken. She now stated, with a very serious note in her voice, "Whatever Mr. Morningstar has experienced, and what is now on that tape, I would say would have to be one of the most heinous, and terrifying experience that has ever happened to any soul, on or off this plane of energy. I am really quite worried about him. In all of my years as a therapist, I have never seen anything so transforming, or right out scary, as this.

"And I really am concerned to the point of Mr. Morningstar harming himself or somebody else. He has been deeply effected by this and may need someone. Do you know where his cabin is?"

"Yes, I do," I answered. "What are you proposing, Maggie?"

"Maybe you and Billy should drive by and see if he is home, maybe he will want to see somebody now."

"We can sure give it a try, Maggie," I assured her. "We will go see him and see where his head is at now. God I can sure see now why he called it the creature."

"You got that one right," agreed Billy.

Donnie's cabin was up on the bench, which was approximately 4 to 5 miles up the approach to the summit of Big Bear Mountain's final peak. We cruised up in the Lincoln, Billy driving. No one spoke, we were both in deep thought due to our recent experience with the mystic.

"That's it ahead on the left, Billy," I said, "drive on up the driveway, Donnie usually parks behind." We drove cautiously up to the log cabin that was almost hidden by the thick growth of ponderosa pines that surrounded it. The driveway circled the log cabin and came back together in front. There was no Chevy pickup. I checked the doors, they were both locked. And an eerie silence seemed to engulf the place.

"I think, Billy, that we should head for the Crazy Horse, Donnie just might have headed over there."

"Okay," answered Billy, looking rather disturbed, "let's go over there, he sure as hell ain't around this spooky place."

"Oh," I said, "you got that feeling too, did you? I thought that maybe it was just my imagination acting up, after our recent experience with, whatever the hell you want to call it. But this place definitely is giving me the creeps too."

We headed back down the gravel road, and back to the Big Bear strip.

The Crazy Horse was operating at its peak. Hank Williams Senior could be heard above this wild and drunken crowd. He was giving us, "My Son Calls Another Man Daddy." The place was crowded and very loud. I found Guy and quickly briefed him on what had come down with Morningstar.

"Is that right, is that right," he kept repeating, as I told him what had happened.

"We went up and checked his cabin, but finding it deserted we thought maybe he had come down here."

"No, no, he hasn't shown his face around here," said Guy excitedly. "Well I'll be damned," he stated, "well I'll be damned. You guys stopping for a beer?" he asked.

"Yes, if we can find a place to take a load off," I said.

"Far end of the bar," said Guy, and hurried away with his full tray of beer.

"I think we had better have a couple of shooters," shouted Billy over the uproar, "if we are going to have any chance of fitting in here."

I agreed, and the barmaid responded with, "Fircwater twice?"

"That's right," I told her, "we are trying to get back on the band wagon."

I checked my wrist clock, just past midnight. "Jesus," I said, "the time is flying, I'm going to step out to the Lincoln and call Maggie on the cell phone. She will be wondering about us and also about Donnie."

"Okay," answered Billy, "I'll hold the fort."

Maggie was relieved to know where we were, and to at least know of nothing negative happening to Donnie. "When are you coming home?" she asked.

"Soon," I answered.

"Okay," said Maggie, "I'm going to stay with Aunt Betsey, you and Billy can have the motor home to yourselves."

"Okay, Maggie, I will see you in the morning, good night now."

It was now 2 a.m. Fat Billy had taken up with a fairly attractive blonde from Los Angeles named Linda. She was approximately

40 years of age, a bit chubby, but seemed very pleasant and sociable. Billy was already at the courting stage, and the bullshit was just too thick for me. As everything that was coming off of Billy's silver tongue was laced heavily with barefaced lies and deceit. And Linda, poor girl, was soaking everything up with a wide smile of nothing but admiration.

I got up and said, "See you two love birds in a bit." I walked over to the bar where Guy was drawing beers for the barmaids.

"What time are you shutting down, Guy?" I asked over the roar of the crowd.

"Two-thirty," Guy shouted back, "but it will take till three to get 'em all to hell out of here. Stick around, Ter, I want to talk with you when things quiet down."

"Okay with me," I assured him, and headed back to our table.

Billy and Linda were now in a tight embrace. Sharing a serious, and I would imagine, slobbery kiss. Another lady sat down as Bill and Linda came up for air. She was a friend of Linda's from Los Angeles. She was very attractive, slender and brown, with long black hair. She introduced herself with the comment, "These two are too far gone to introduce me, they think that they are the only two here." She smiled showing beautiful even white teeth.

"My name is Conchita," she said, and extended a slender hand.

I took her hand graciously and told her that I was Terry Fraser. And that I was down from Canada for an extended period of time.

"Oh, how long is your visa for?" she asked politely.

"What visa are you referring to, Conchita?" I asked. "As a matter of fact, what is a visa?"

"Yes, you are my kind of man all right," she said, as we both shared a hearty laugh.

Guy was now on the loud speaker. "Drink up, ladies and

gentlemen, it's time to go home. You got fifteen minutes to drink up, off sales are at the end of the bar. Let's go, folks, let's go, we want to go home too."

Billy now informed me that he wanted to drive the girls back to their hotel. Conchita seemed to have somehow got the idea that I was available, and had linked her arm in mine and randomly rested her head on my shoulder.

"Yes, would you guys mind seeing us home, we walked down here from the Big Bear Hotel," stated Linda. "We were out for a midnight stroll when we heard all of the activity in here, and I sure am glad I did. Just look at what I have found," she shouted joyously, as she gave Fat Billy a peck on the cheek.

Yes, just look at what you have found, I laughed to myself.

"You girls got any beer at your hotel?" asked Billy, always thinking about his stomach.

"Yes, we got beer and coolers," said Conchita. "You're coming, aren't you?" she asked, and gave me a peck on the cheek.

"Yes, we can see you lovely ladies home all right," I told her, "but I have to see Guy for a moment before I go. So no hurry with the drinks."

The Crazy Horse was emptying out very quickly now. In a few minutes we were the only patrons left in this notorious room.

Guy came over with a fresh round of drinks on his tray. "Man, what a night," he yawned, "I'm totally beat. What I want to tell you, Ter," said Guy behind his wide yawn. "I have been thinking it over about Morningstar, and I will personally bet that he headed down to San Bernardino. There is a group of the elders, of the Apache Nation down there. And I think he has gone on down to approach them with this problem. And to seek advice. They are governed by visions and messages from their higher power, you know. They will straighten him out, and he will come back when he is ready."

"That all makes perfect sense, Guy," I told him. "And thanks for taking the time to enlighten me. Maggie, most of all, will be very appreciative to hear this." We drank up and bid Guy a final good night.

The two girls had an expensive suite on the second floor. Complete with two bedrooms and a kitchenette. Fat Billy, his mind on one thing and one thing only, had taken Linda to the bedroom almost immediately upon arrival. And as a matter of fact, the moans and ooos and aaas were very quickly becoming a part of the décor.

Conchita and I sipped a cold one. She told me she was of the Navajo Nation. City raised in L.A., where she worked as a model. She had taken quite a liking to me, and was letting me know it with touches and glances that told me that there was still more of tonight to come, if that was what we wanted. I did think about Maggie, and I made a quick decision. She was at Aunt Betsy's for the night, and what she didn't know, I thought, wouldn't hurt her. The many drinks of the night were taking their toll on me, along with the many charms of this beautiful Navajo princess. After all I am only human. Conchita, by this time, was parading around the kitchen in just her scanty underpants and bra. There was no turning back now. Soon our bedroom had joined chorus with Billy and Linda's. The moans and groans now just a common subject to our ears.

My subconscious mind woke me. I checked my wrist clock, it was 5 a.m. I had to move fast now and get back to the motor home, before Maggie woke up and got out of her bed at Auntie's. Conchita was sleeping peacefully and soundly. I slipped out of bed silently, threw on my clothes, and carrying my shoes, let myself out soundlessly.

I climbed into bed in the motor home. It was five-thirty a.m. I fell into an immediate and deep sleep. The next thing I heard was Maggie's sweet voice.

"Wake up, you nighthawk," she said pleasantly. "What happened to Fat Billy?"

CHAPTER TEN

FAT BILLY LEAVES BIG BEAR

"Oh, that poor soul," I said sleepily, "Morningstar scalped him last night."

"What!!!" screamed Maggie. "What did you say!!!"

I took one look at Maggie's beautiful face contorted in anguish and I knew that I had better fix things fast. "No, no, Maggie," I said quickly, jumping out of bed and embracing her. "I was only kidding, guess I was still half asleep," I said in apology. "No the fat man found himself a blonde at the Crazy Horse last night. I dropped them off at the Big Bear Hotel after the Crazy Horse closed up."

"Oh, thank God," she said. "Thank God, and don't you ever do ever do that again. I feel somewhat responsible for the state of mind that Mr. Morningstar is now in, you know," stated Maggie, with a grave expression.

"Don't you worry, Maggie, don't you worry about Morningstar," I said, as I tried to comfort her. And then I told her what Guy had thought about his whereabouts. And Maggie also now agreed that it made perfect sense. That was the place that the troubled man would definitely be.

"I feel better now," stated the beautiful lady. Her face had taken on that, I'm-in-charge look again.

"How is Aunt Betsey?" I asked Maggie. "I haven't seen her for three or four days. Ask her if she wants to see a Robert Mitchum movie tonight, being as it is Sunday and all."

"I'll tell you what," laughed Maggie, "the answer is definitely yes, and I haven't even asked her yet, can we do it at eight. Auntie likes to be in bed by ten, you know."

"We sure can," I agreed. "I'll go pick up Billy in awhile and I can get the movie then."

"Okay," said the beautiful lady, putting her arm around my waist. "You come for breakfast now, Auntie is cooking."

One look at Aunt Betsy's wood-burning chimney definitely confirmed her statement. We headed for the log house, happily, and arm in arm.

We passed the remainder of the morning on Aunt Betsy's porch. My stomach was busy digesting the beautifully cooked ham, eggs, brown toast, and blackberry jam. My cell phone rang, startling me out of my state of grandiose.

"I bet I know who that is," smiled Maggie.

"Yes," I agreed, "I know that you know, even I know," I said amusedly. "And a good afternoon to you, Billy," I said into the cell phone.

The fat man's voice boomed joyously over the wire. "How about coming down and picking me up?" he asked.

"Sure will," I assured him. "Be down in 5 minutes."

I climbed the stairs to the second floor of the Big Bear Hotel. It was Sunday all right, the building was quiet and serene. I knocked on door #216.

"Come on in, you're out," came the booming voice of Fat Billy. He was in complete charge now I thought, and smiled to myself. I opened the door and was greeted with.

"Well hello. Where did you go? What time did you leave?" Conchita was doing the asking. She wore an expression somewhere between disapproval that I had left, and pleasure that I was back again. Billy was right in his glory, and grinning from ear to ear. He was in charge all right. He was reclined in a recliner, surrounded by Linda. She was dressed in a bikini and was serving him food and drinks. Conchita also sported a scanty red bikini, which brought back to mind, those stolen moments of bliss of yesternight. I gave her my best smile and saw that it was working. She grabbed me in those hungry and pretty arms of hers, and kissed me lingeringly on the lips.

"Some of us have got to get up early and do things," I explained to her.

"I didn't think that you would miss me for a short while." I smiled at her pretty Navajo face.

"Yes, I did miss you," she pouted, "and now that I'm awake you are not going to get away."

"Ho, ho, ho," laughed Billy. "You've had it now, Ter. Don't get her on the warpath," he hollered gleefully.

"No, no, I don't want to do that," I said. "One Indian on the warpath is quiet sufficient for one weekend." We all shared a hearty laugh. The girls not understanding the joke, but laughing anyway, just because they were happy.

I had been quite relaxed the night before with the situation between Maggie and Conchita. As Maggie was asleep at Aunt Betsy's. And like I said, not knowing is not hurting anyone. But today I was feeling a little uneasy faced with this gorgeous, possessive Navajo Princess. I don't know if any of you readers out there have ever experienced what I'm about to tell you. But I'm sure some of you will agree with me on this.

Due to past experience I have learned that a possessive woman, who has been made even a bit suspicious of her territory being invaded, seems to possess a sixth sense. I have no idea where the information gets funneled from. But it does get funneled to them through some channel that us, the defendant, is unable to tap into. Or even to be able to know, where to tap in.

They will, in fact, just know that you have had relations with someone else. And I have even experienced the uncomfortable situation of being tracked down in another woman's house by a possessive girlfriend. When I knew for a fact that it was an impossibility for her to know of my whereabouts through any explainable reason. I swear that she had this sixth sense.

Like a pet dog that will cross a state, or even a continent, to be with its family that has moved, and for whatever reason, left the dog behind. I also compared her to a "homing pigeon." Me being home. As I now looked eye to eye with this pretty Navajo. All these feelings that I have just explained to you, began drifting through my conscious mind.

"What's the matter?" she asked. Seemingly reading my expression, or possibly my mind.

The moment was saved by the fat man's silver tongue. "He's just sad because we have to go, that's all, Conchita," Billy told her gently. Both girls now snapped out of their little pleasure trance.

"GO!!! Have to go," they chorused. "You didn't say anything about going anywhere, Billy," said Linda, looking a little forlorn. "I thought that you guys lived here, and we got a whole two weeks holidays, you knew that, you big heartbreaking party pooper."

Conchita was quiet, as I hadn't exactly promised her the moon last night. As I'm sure that Billy had promised Linda. Linda now physically cuffed Billy alongside the head. And made a dash for the bedroom, slamming the door behind her.

Fat Billy, completely unruffled, now turned his charming smile on Conchita and I. "What time we going, Ter?" he asked indifferently.

And to add insult to injury, I answered firmly, "Right about now, comrades, right about now."

Conchita, more in possession of her faculties than the lovesick Linda, took my arm and said, "Come with me." She led me into the bedroom where we had made such harmony last night, closing the door behind us.

"How long are you going to be away? And do you want me to be here for you when you get back?" asked the pretty lady.

The answers to her questions came from my expression of "the easy way out." I would be back on the weekend, Saturday, and yes, I certainly did want her to be there when I got back.

Those pretty brown arms were now around me. And the red bikini fell gracefully to the floor, as we entered another hour of rapture. And by the moans and the groans, coming from the other bedroom. I could tell that Fat Billy had been accepted back into paradise.

"Thought I would have to go looking for you two," stated Maggie, and not completely with her usual pleasant attitude.

Oh God, I thought to myself. The memories of the lost dog and the homing pigeon were rushing through my mind like it was yesterday.

"Had quite a time getting this big lug away from Linda," I answered. Shifting the onus completely onto the fat man. *After all he had started it all*, I thought, justifying myself at the same time.

"I'm ashamed of you, Billy," stated Maggie sternly. "You leave little Sylvia back in Desert Hot Springs with all those children, and then you run around on her, that's disgusting." And after a moment, and much to my dismay, she added, "If Terry was to pull such a stunt on me, I would scalp him, so help me God." I felt my scalp creep as my guilty complex was disturbed for a moment.

The moment was again saved by the fat man's silver tongue.

"No, no, no," blurted Billy. Acting like he had just been highly insulted. "You're looking at it entirely opposite to what the situation really is."

Maggie turned to him. I could see that her beautiful face was now crimson with anger. Very unlike her. "Explain," she stated flatly.

The fat man, now seeing how serious this situation had become, was now on his feet. Putting on his best performance, with hand gestures. And I'm telling you nothing but the truth expression. He explained to the angry Maggie. "You see, pretty woman, if I was to stay around Desert Hot Springs with Sylvia and the kids all the time, it would be my nature to become bored with life. And when I get bored I get this miserable streak that not only makes me miserable, but everybody else around me also becomes miserable. And I can't help it, Maggie." Billy was now down on one knee, his performance was excellent. "I have tried to help it, but there are just so many things in our life that we are able to control. And if you think for one minute, that I don't love Sylvia, and my gorgeous little children, then, Maggie, you are badly mistaken." There were now tears running down both sides of fat Billy's cheeks. "I did this for them, Maggie, not for me, Maggie, but for my family." The word "family" came out with a sob. Billy was now down on both knees and sobbing openly. And if I hadn't have known what a rascal he truly was, I think I would have cried too. What an act.

The soft-hearted Maggie was now completely free from her anger. She was in fact, almost in tears herself. She walked over to where Billy was kneeling and crying openly and loudly. She touched his shoulder and comforted him with, "It's okay, Billy, it's okay, don't cry. I understand you now, it's all right. Come on, get up and come sit with Terry at the table."

Billy sat down across from me wiping his tears with the towel that Maggie had given him. As Maggie went into the motor home to get us a beer and put Elvis Presley on, the fat man gave me a tearful wink. And an expression of "How was that for a performance?" It was all either of us could do to keep from busting out in laughter. But Fat Billy knowing what thin ice he was skating on, kept a straight face and thanked Maggie humbly for the beer.

I called the Maverick Bus Lines on the cell phone. Billy's bus was leaving in 25 minutes.

"That's real good," stated Billy. "I'm tired, I'll sleep all the way down to Desert Hot Springs. The motion of the bus always makes me sleepy anyway. Even when I haven't been awake for three days," he added with a grin.

Fat Billy boarded the bus with a "I'll see you next Saturday, Ter."

My feelings were a little mixed. I didn't really know if I wanted another performance, so soon or not. But I didn't give him a bad answer.

I stopped off and got Aunt Betsy's Robert Mitchum movie. It was called, *The River of No Return.* And was the first Hollywood cast to be done entirely in Canada. Being done in year 1956. The movie was very good.

It starred Marilyn Monroe with Mitchum, and also co-starred Rory Calhoun. Before running the movie I sat down with Aunt Betsey and related to her some true and interesting history that happened during the production of this movie. And especially with Auntie being such a Robert Mitchum fan, I knew that she just had to hear of his true-life episode in the Canadian Rockies.

After completing a day of casting, Robert Mitchum was relaxing with some of his coworkers over a few beers. In the town of Banff, Alberta, where the movie was being shot. "The River of No Return," being the Bow River that flows through Banff, Alberta. After a few beers Mitchum decided to take a drive up towards Lake Louise. Which is on #1 highway, going west from Banff. Robert was driving a new 1956 Ford Thunderbird. A model that the collectors will now give their eyeteeth for. The top was down on the Thunderbird. The highway was clear and dry, and Robert was feeling his beers. So he decided to test the little T-Bird for acceleration and handling. He was now whipping down #1, at 80 and 90 miles per hour.

Unfortunately he met an oncoming RCMP highway patrol car. Noticing his high rate of speed and recognizing the driver as Mitchum, these two rookies decided to turn around and pull him over, and get some recognition for themselves. This cruiser made a U-turn, and was now engaged in a high-speed pursuit of Mitchum and his T-Bird. After several breath-taking miles, with speeds in excess of 100 miles per hour. They were tight on the rear of the T-Bird, with flashers and sirens in full swing.

Mitchum pulled over. The two officers got out of the cruiser and approached the T-Bird. Robert was asked to get out of his car and walk the white highway line, as a test for his sobriety to operate a motor vehicle. After failing this test. At least to the eyes of these two rookies, Robert was informed that he was under arrest, for speeding and impaired driving. And was ordered to get in the back seat of the highway cruiser.

Now Mitchum in 1956 was big and strong. And being in his prime, he had other ideas about how he was riding back to Banff. Not being able to make a compromise with these overly anxious officers, Mitchum took the only other alternative. Two well-delivered right punches, and two of the Queen's best were sprawled on the side of the highway, alongside their cruiser. Robert Mitchum was now making a U-turn in the T-Bird, and was on his way back to Banff.

The end result of this episode, which was very big news in Canada in 1956, and was in fact, headline news in the *Calgary Herald*, never did see Mitchum arrested. This being due to his celebrity status. And also due to the fact that Canada wanted Hollywood on the north side of the Canadian border. End result. Robert was served with a court summons to appear, and paid a stiff fine. Which would be peanuts to a man of Mitchum's caliber. I have often wondered about those two rookie officers. Did they ever go to see the movie, *River of No Return*?

Aunt Betsey was on the edge of her seat. "That devil," she muttered, with a look of disapproval. But she wasn't fooling me, I saw that glitter in the corner of her eyes. That told me the true tale, of how Auntie was feeling about Robert's Rocky Mountain episode.

CHAPTER ELEVEN

BUSINESS IN BIG BEAR CITY

Always being a hard worker, I had decided that it was time to go back to work. Also I knew that my bank account needed attention. Being as Big Bear didn't offer much more than a weekly town rag, in the way of advertisement at our disposal, I took another approach to the problem. I bought myself a one-ton cube van that had been advertised on the bulletin board on the outside wall of the Crazy Horse. Being as this truck's enclosed cargo box offered an advertisement space of 8 foot by 12 foot on each side, I hired an old semiretired sign painter, a friend of Guy's, to paint some advertisements for me. When finished, each side of the cargo van spoke to the crowd very loudly. With bright red and black letters on white, 12 inches high, saying loud and clear: "Terry Fraser General Contracting. Stone Retaining Walls and Waterfalls. A Complete Lawn Care Service." Signed off of course with my cell phone number.

As soon as the paint was dry, Maggie and I cruised the strip, setting the first day of our advertisement into motion. After a two-hour tour, I left the truck parked in front of the Big Bear Hotel. Where it could be left safely for the night. Maggie and

I decided to barhop our way home on foot. We went into one of the many saloons on our homeward route. Just then my cell phone rang, and it was for business. I crossed over to the convenience store and bought a pen and pad. By the time we reached the motor home, we had 17 calls. That included everything from, removing a tree, to building a waterfall, to lawn cutting.

"Business is booming, Maggie dear," I remarked.

"And how!" was her reply.

All these calls I made an appointment for over the next three days.

My days now became busy and long. I bought brush cutters, lawn mowers, wheelbarrows, etc. I hired two Mexican wetbacks for labor, and a stonemason from North Dakota. Things were good. The customers were all rich millionaires from Palm Springs and Los Angeles. And the money began to flow my way.

Saturday came, it was just past noon and we were finishing a tree removal job. Fat Billy hadn't called to say that he would be up. And I felt somewhat relieved that he hadn't, as I really didn't have time for him now. Conchita, I knew, would be at the Crazy Horse tonight if I wanted to see her. I felt good, everything was going my way. I was healthy. I was free. I was making money. And also surrounded by beautiful women. The gods were indeed smiling down on me. One thing that I have always prided myself in, I never forgot my place in society. Instead of taking times like this for granted, like I have seen a lot of other people do, and becoming self-centered and conceited, I always remembered that I was still that same farm boy with a grade school education. The only thing that was different was my circumstances, which I counted as my daily blessings. And I always, on a daily basis, kept in touch with my "Great Creator." To whom I give thanks for granting me the strength and intelligence, to position myself as I was and am.

My employees, which amounted to 6 now, fully understood that the Crazy Horse was my main business headquarters. And if they wanted their paychecks, they should be there at 2 a.m. Saturday afternoon. My Mexican wetbacks had now multiplied to 5. They were great workers who held me on a god-like pedestal, as I was allowing them to work for me without a green card. And since they were illegal immigrants, I always paid them the basic wage in cash each week, as I knew that they didn't have a bank account. These Mexican wetbacks had taken up residence, as squatters, in a rambling old building, which had been a roadhouse and a notorious whorehouse, of the bustling gold mining days of Big Bear Mountain. The old building was in a sad state of affairs. But it was summertime and they didn't really need much in the way of shelter. This old roadhouse was located beside Little Bear (dry lake). But on the other side of the highway, and far enough out of town that the law didn't bother them. Their main, and only source of water, was that artisan water vein jet. Where I had got water to cool the radiator of the Lincoln, a few weeks prior. And on my first introduction to Big Bear Mountain.

There were 18 of these Mexican people in all, staying at the old roadhouse. The five men who worked for me, and the remainder being women and children, of all ages and sizes. Only 1 out of the 5 of the Mexicans, who were in my employment, spoke broken English. And so I made him labor foreman, interpreter, etc. How they had gotten smuggled across the U.S. border and arrived in Big Bear, I have not the faintest idea. And never asked. The one Mexican who was fortunate enough to speak a little English was a very likeable man. I would say he was 32 years of age, and very intelligent. His name was Ali.

I was now sitting at a table facing this same Ali in the Crazy Horse Saloon. The other four Mexicans were all seated around the table also. It was their first payday from me. And possibly their first since leaving Mexico. Ali had 3 days pay coming, three of the others had 2 days, and one had only one day. But being as they were living as a commune, they now had all of the money that was required for their simple needs.

Ali, with his fist full of American bills that I had just given him, was asking me in his broken English if he could pay me to drive them out to the old roadhouse that they called home. He wanted to drop the others off, and then take his wife Viola, into the Big Bear grocery to get supplies. As they were all quite hungry, I assured them that we could do this, as soon as Tim, the stonemason, came in and got his paycheck.

Guy brought us a round of beer. He looked at Ali, a puzzled expression was on his face. "This is Ali, Guy. Ali, Guy." I introduced them.

"I know you from somewhere," stated Guy.

"I don't know you," stated Ali, in his broken English.

"It will come to me," stated Guy, "just give me time."

"Must be mistake," said Ali, "this first time in America."

Guy left it at that and walked away, that puzzled expression still deep on his face. Tim the stonemason popped in, but didn't want to stay for a beer.

I gave him his paycheck and he departed with a hearty "See you on Monday."

"Okay, boys," I said, "let's drink up and I will see you home."

They all piled into the cube van. Each with a 24 flat of beer clutched in their hands, and a smile a mile wide. We pulled into the old roadhouse and were immediately surrounded with women and children of all sizes and ages. Ali was shouting orders, right and left. A very attractive Mexican woman came over to us.

"This is Viola," said Ali. "Viola, meet Mr. Fraser, our friend and work boss."

Viola bowed to me, which was their custom, and said in almost perfect English, "I am so very pleased to meet you, Mr. Fraser, I have already heard so much about you."

I was becoming flattered with all of the attention that I was getting. Most of the kids surrounded us and were all trying to talk to me at the same time. Viola shooed them away.

"I am very surprised, and very pleased with your ability to speak the English language," I told her.

"Oh," she said, "I grew up in a rich gringo's home in Mexico City, my mother was their housekeeper, and that's where I learned to speak the lingo," she said, and smiled warmly at me.

"I'm ready to go shopping any time you are," I said to Ali.

"We ready now," he answered.

The grocery store was right across the road from the Crazy Horse. So I parked the van right next to the grocery exit. I left it unlocked and told Ali to come and get me in the bar when they were ready to go.

The first thing that Guy said to me when I walked into the Crazy Horse was, "Where is that Mex from, Ter? I just know that I know him from somewhere."

"Just another wetback, Guy. First time that he has been out of Mexico, so he tells me. Did you ever spend anytime in Mexico City?" I asked him.

"No," said Guy, "I have never been there."

"You must have him mixed up with some other dude," I said.

Guy looked at me, that same puzzled expression still on his face. "I don't think so," he said slowly. "I never forget a face. And how come he speaks English, if this is his first time out of Mexico?" Guy asked suspiciously.

"He learned it from his wife," I said. "She grew up in a rich gringo's house in Mexico City, her mother being the head housekeeper there for many years."

"Well, that certainly explains why he speaks some English all right," admitted Guy. But I could see that he wasn't ready to drop it. "That Mex's face is going to bother me until I figure this out," he remarked, very serious now.

"He will be over in a bit to get me," I said. "He and his wife Viola are grocery shopping across the street, why don't you come and talk to him some more," I suggested.

"No," said Guy, "I don't want to make him feel uncomfortable, him being a wetback and all, his life is probably difficult enough without me poking into his affairs. It will all come to me, Ter," Guy said patiently now. "Just give me a bit of time, and I guarantee you I saw that Mexican's face before. And it must have been something damned important for me to remember it this well. And it must have been a long time ago."

"Well, the man is only in his early thirties," I told him.

"I know," said Guy. "And that only makes matters more confusing." He gave me a grin and went back to work.

Ali came over to my table. "Got food now, boss," he stated with a grin, "maybe we now can go, Viola feed babies."

We got in the cube van. Viola was in the back with a huge pile of provisions. "Ali," I asked, "what do you have in that old roadhouse for furnishings?"

"Just blankets to sleep on," he stated, "and now food."

"Okay," I said, "we are going to make one more stop."

We pulled up in front of the "Mountain Secondhand Store." The same store where Maggie and I had purchased the furnishings for under our canopy. I took Ali inside with me, where I purchased 2 large kitchen tables, twenty assorted chairs, some constructed of wood, some of metal. Also one naphtha gas camp stove, complete with a 2 gallon can of naphtha gas, and 2 gas lanterns.

"Okay, Ali," I said, "let's get this stuff on the truck."

This was a little too much in one day for Ali. I could see the tears forming in his dark eyes.

"It's okay, Ali," I said cheerfully. I explained what the overall cost of the furnishings came to, and that I would be deducting from his pay each week, until the debt was settled.

"That okay?"

"That wonderful," was his quiet comment.

I backed the van up to the rickety front porch of the ancient roadhouse. We got the lanterns out and got them fired up. Ali was shouting orders again and the food and furnishings seemed to magically transfer from truck to roadhouse. The atmosphere in the old roadhouse that night was one of extreme happiness and gayety. Of which I felt so deeply, I will remember it always. The men now gathered by the lantern light.

They had brought their musical instruments out, and soon we were all enjoying some fine music from Mexico. As only the Mexicans can play it. There were 4 flutes, 1 violin, 3 mandolins, and 1 Hawaiian guitar. I sat at Ali's new table and soaked up this beautiful music, which I had never heard played as well. It was an awesome little party. The women were now feeding the children.

"I have to go now, Ali," I said. I headed for the door amid a chorus of Mexican farewells. I climbed into the van and headed for home.

It was close to midnight and I hadn't had the time to make any contact with Maggie that entire day. There was a note taped to the motor home door. I ripped it off and took it inside where I could see to read it.

> Terry, my dear. I sure don't get to see much of you anymore, Aunt Betsey and I became a little bored today, and so have taken the bus down to San Bernardino. Aunty has old friends there and wanted to visit with them, we will return tomorrow, Sunday evening.
>
> I Love You
>
> Maggie.

CHAPTER TWELVE

CONCHITA MOUNTAIN AGAIN

Well, I thought to myself, being as I had just been abandoned. *I might as well go down to the Crazy Horse, and see what is unfolding down there tonight. Or I guess I should say, down there this morning*. As it was now twelve-forty-five. I took a quick shower, changed into clean jeans and T-shirt, fired up the Lincoln and was on my way. Crazy Horse bound.

The front door of the saloon was wide open as always, letting escape the relaxing and magical music of the late Jim Reeves. He was giving us, "Put Your Sweet Lips a Little Closer to the Phone." Which I recognized as a 1959 all-time hit. I walked on into the big barroom. The crowd was lively and loud, as usual. I saw some waving hands at the far end of the room, and heard my name being shouted above the rest of the hubbub. Recognizing Conchita and Linda I went on over. I was greeted with a beautiful squeeze, and many kisses from the gorgeous Navajo Princess, Conchita.

"Where is Billy? Where is Billy?" Linda was chiming, with a look of disappointment spreading over her pretty face.

"I don't think that Billy will be able to make it tonight,

Linda," I told her. And seeing her disappointment, I added, "But I'm sure he will be contacting you soon as I am well aware of how much he thinks of you."

"Really?" she chimed. Now with a big smile of relief on her lovesick face.

"Hell yes," I lied, "you're all he ever talks about."

"Well, I better be," she stated. "Anyway we have to go back to L.A. tomorrow, our holidays are over."

She fished a notepad and pen out of her oversized purse, and presented me with her number and address in Los Angeles. With strict orders to make sure that Billy gets it.

"I'll guard it with my life," I told her.

Conchita was leaning against me. Her hand, under the beer table, was creeping up my inner thigh.

"You coming to my place tonight?" she whispered in my ear.

"Wouldn't miss it for the world," I assured her, as her gentle hand now caressed, you know what.

Guy came over with last call on his beer tray and slapped it down on the table.

"You hear anything from Morningstar?" I asked him, shouting above the uproar.

"No," Guy shouted back, "but I'm going down to San Bernardino for tomorrow and Monday, and will try to contact the elders while I am there," he shouted.

"Sounds good," I shouted back. "Be sure to let me know as soon as you have something."

He nodded in agreement. The two girls and I made our way to the Big Bear Hotel. Linda decided to retire, and left Conchita and I in the kitchenette. We too soon followed her example, as the storm was brewing, quickly, and ferociously in our blood streams.

It was high noon before I awoke from my peaceful and overdue night's rest. The two girls were bustling around the suite. Getting everything packed for the trip back to Los Angeles, as their bus was leaving in less than an hour. I helped pack their belongings down to the Lincoln, and drove them to the Maverick Bus Lines. We said our goodbyes very quickly as the bus was already loading. Conchita was in a good frame of mind, and made me promise that I would visit her in Los Angeles, very soon. She left with beautiful backward looks. And blew me a kiss through the bus window.

It was now three months later. The spring had gone by like the wind before the storm. And summer was disappearing just about as fast. I didn't go down to the Crazy Horse much anymore. I was just too damned busy. My contracting business was a booming success, we were literally turning down jobs daily. But I did see Guy every Saturday, as payday at 2 p.m. at the Crazy Horse, was still a standing ovation. Guy had approached the Apache elders on his tip to San Bernardino, but was unable to learn anything about Donnie Morningstar. He told me that the elders had denied seeing him, or even knowing him. This had us all very concerned about Donnie's whereabouts. As approximately 4 months had now passed since his session with Maggie and his disappearance. This was something that I could see really bothered Maggie, each and every day.

The Mexicans now had one truck amongst them. It was an older model Chevy pickup that they had purchased from one of the locals for $300. It wasn't in too bad of condition, and was doing the job, as far as meeting the little tribe's transportation needs. The old roadhouse now bragged 4 overstuffed, old-fashioned chesterfields, and countless inflatable mattresses.

Maggie and I had made it a point to stop off at the old roadhouse and visit with these people at least once every week or two. Viola and Maggie soon became real close friends. Upon seeing that they could enjoy a visit so well, I would make sure that we stopped in Saturday evenings for a couple of hours. Maggie enjoying the fine Mexican music as much as I did. Ali was an excellent host and both Maggie and myself were completely relaxed and uninhibited in the company of these simple people. I saw them as a grateful group, with the happiest bunch of children that I have ever met. But unfortunately, and without any of us knowing it that night, Ali's seemingly blissful existence was about to be threatened.

CHAPTER THIRTEEN

BIG BEAR CITY'S GREAT GOLD ROBBERY

It was now the first week in September. I was outside enjoying the sunrise, and I could feel the autumn nip in the air, as it hinted to us of the approaching winter ahead. Just then my cell phone rang. I looked at my wrist clock, only six-forty-five. Who the hell could this be so early?

"Hello," I said.

"Hello, Terry," Guy barked, with a note of real urgency in his voice.

"I'm down in the bar and got the coffee on. I just got back from Los Angeles and San Bernardino. And I got something real damned important that I think you better have a look at with me. Come on down and I will let you in the side door."

Noting the urgency in his voice, and figuring that maybe it had something to do with the disappearance of Morningstar, I answered, "Be right down, Guy, keep the coffee hot."

I stepped into the motor home to get my car keys. Maggie was now awake and asked, "Where you off to this early, Terry?"

I briefed her on Guy's already brief message, and suggested

that it might have something to do with Morningstar.

"Please call me as soon as you find out," she said, "you know how worried I am about the whereabouts of Mr. Morningstar."

"I will, Maggie." I gave her a hug, and a kiss on her pretty lips.

"Just be patient," I said, and headed for the Crazy Horse.

I wrapped on the side door, it burst open as soon as my knuckles hit it. Guy was really waiting for me.

"I told you so!" he was shouting. At first I thought he was half drunk, but soon saw that it was just his excitement.

"Told me what, Guy? What are you hollering about?" I asked him calmly.

Guy was shaking a piece of newsprint in front of my face, and said, still almost shouting, "Come over to the table, grab a coffee and have a look at this."

I poured a coffee and sat down at the table beside the reading light.

"I told you that I had seen that Mex's face before, now didn't I?" said Guy, a bit calmer. "And I also told you it must have been a long time ago, now didn't I?"

"Yes, you sure did," I answered, and I now started to feel some real curiosity.

"Well," said Guy, shouting again, "just take a look at this," and he slapped the newsprint down on the table in front of me. I looked down, and to my great surprise, there staring up at me was the face of Ali.

"Jesus, Guy," I muttered, "what the hell's going on here? This San Bernardino newsprint is dated July 10, 1898. This god damned news is 90 years old. What the hell is going on? The Ali I know is only 35 years old. This is year 1988."

"Yes, yes, I know," stated Guy, still shouting with excitement, "but read the story, read the god damned story."

I brought out my eyeglasses for this, and started at the top of the page under the 1898 date. The headlines went like this:

DARING DAYLIGHT GOLD SHIPMENT ROBBERY NETS THIEVES THREE HUNDRED THOUSAND IN GOLD BULLION

A shipment of refined gold was being transferred from the cyanide gold refinery in Big Bear City on Monday, July 8, 1898. It was being transferred by a Wells Fargo armored wagon, to San Bernardino. Where it was to be put aboard the southbound rail train. And from there it was designated for the California Gold Mint, in Los Angeles.

At approximately two miles south of Big Bear City, this armored wagon in mention, was blown to pieces by these daring desperadoes. It seems like a large charge of dynamite was buried in the center of the gravel road. And when the armored wagon drove over it, the charge was then set off by one of the bandits, who was concealed somewhere in the trees. The charge broke the four-horse team free, which stampeded them down the road in the direction of San Bernardino. The wagon floor was blown out, allowing the gold to fall to the road. The driver and shotgun guard were both killed in the blast, as was also the guard riding inside of the armored unit.

A suspect, who was spotted and identified by an ex-miner turned trapper and hunter, has been arrested. He was spotted by this trapper within a quarter-mile of the robbery site, shortly after the eruption of the dynamite blast that killed these three Wells Fargo men. The man pictured is Adrian Recinos. He was arrested early yesterday morning, without incident. At his roadhouse called the Black Betsey, which is situated north of Big Bear City, near Little Bear Lake. This man is now being held on suspicion of grand theft, and three counts of murder one. If convicted he faces the hangman.

"The Black Betsey," I muttered. "The Black Betsey beside Little Bear Lake. Why that's the old roadhouse where Ali is now squatting, well I'll be damned."

"Yes, Ter," said Guy excitedly. "Old Adrian Recinos is pictured here, he is the guy who built the Black Betsey. And sold moonshine and whores to the gold miners and drifters. Apparently it was quite a place in its day. Richly furnished, with a real live Mexican music band and all," said Guy. "Old Adrian Recinos had a son, and a couple of daughters. And do you know where that cyanide gold refinery sat?"

"No I haven't the faintest," I said.

"Well, I want to tell you, that pile of ruble up on the hill behind the Black Betsey, that's all that's left of it. That old Mex knew everything that came and went in that refinery."

"Just a minute now, Guy," I said with genuine interest, "where does Ali now fit into the picture?"

"Well, there is only two possible ways that he could fit in," said Guy firmly. "He's either the great grandson, or he's the reincarnation of old Adrian Recinos. I would say that he is the great grandson. And I ought to know, I went to school with his father. That's where I recognized him from, the memory of his father's face, from way back in the 1940s. He looks enough like his father for me to recognize him after all of these years. But as you can see by the news photo, he's the spitting image of his great granddaddy."

"Yes," I said, "I can sure see what you mean, all right. And I would say that Ali's squatter's rights are a lot stronger than what I realized."

"Yes," smiled old Guy, "I guess he has a right to be there if anybody does."

"Well, what happened to the old granddaddy?" I asked.

"Here," said Guy, "it's here somewhere, I got it all. Oh, here it is. This is the *San Bernardino Tribune*, dated a year after his arrest, August 10, 1899."

> Adrian Recinos was arraigned today in the High Court of California, in the city of Los Angeles. Charged with grand theft of a gold shipment on its way to the mint in Los

> Angeles, and the murder of three Wells Fargo security guards. Mr. Recinos was set free this evening from the San Bernardino county jail. Where he had been held for over a year awaiting trial. Mr. Recinos was freed on the clause of, "Lack of Evidence."

"And you know what else, Ter?" said Guy in a half whisper. "That $300,000 in gold bullion has never been found. Take a look at this," he said, as he rummaged through the old newsprints, selecting one and handing it to me. It was the *San Bernardino Tribune* again, dated December 10,1910.

The headlines were: "WHERE IS THE GOLD?"

> The passing life of one of one of the residents of Big Bear City takes the secret to the grave. Mr. Recinos was shot to death in the early hours of December 10, 1910. During an argument at his well-known roadhouse: The Black Betsey. Situated on the north side of Big Bear City.
>
> Mr. Recinos was arrested and held in the San Bernardino county jail eleven years ago. He was charged with the Wells Fargo robbery of $300,000 in gold bullion, from an armored wagon that was blown to pieces by a dynamite charge. Also he was charged with the murder of three Wells Fargo security guards. Although released a year later, due to lack of evidence, it is still thought by the FBI that Mr. Recinos was in fact the guilty party. He had been watched extensively for the past ten years, but failed to give these officers any clues in the whereabouts of this lost fortune in gold bullion. Perhaps the mysterious location of this fortune hunter's dream has gone to the grave forever. "May God Rest His Soul."
>
> San Bernardino Tribune, December 10, 1910.

"And after the old man was shot," Guy went on, "his killer was charged, found guilty, and was hanged in Los Angeles approximately two years after the shooting. The shooting had come about due to one of the whores being beaten by this man. And old Recinos, being the owner of the establishment, had intervened to protect the whore, and lost his own life in the attempt.

"Apparently his son tried to make a go of the place. But the big gold rush was over by that time around Big Bear City. And the business just wasn't there no more. This guy, old Adrian's son, got killed in a mine cave-in shortly after the roadhouse business had shut down. And his son, Berni, who would be Ali's father, abandoned the old place. And after he and I finished grade school, his mother and his two sisters, Rosi and Viola, all headed back to Mexico. And that would be forty years ago now," said Guy reminiscently.

"After that the Black Betsy really went to the dogs. People broke in. The furniture got lugged away. The windows got broken out. And for a few years, treasure hunters came from near and far, to dig up the yard and surrounding acreage, in search of that pile of bullion. But that illusive gold still remains a mystery. And somehow, Ter, I just know that Ali friend of yours is here to retrieve it. I just bet that smart little Mex has some clue as to where it lays, just waiting to be dug up."

Guy's face was now set in hard lines, as he said, "Now listen, Ter, I have brought you all this information, and this Ali guy is a friend of yours. So if we are smart and work together on this, there is no reason why we can't come up with a nice big chunk of it."

"Well, Guy," I said slowly, "this is all quite sudden, give me a little time to mull it over and get the facts straight in my mind."

"Okay, Ter," said Guy impatiently. "But don't take too long, or I will have to act on my own."

"Just be patient for a day or two, Guy," I said, "after all that gold has been out there for over 90 years, so I don't see where a day or two will make much difference now."

"All right," said Guy, still in a state of excitement. "But get back to me god damned soon, Ter, I know when to act, and this is the time."

"I will, Guy," I promised, and headed back to share this tantalizing story with Maggie.

"This is so interesting," she said in astonishment. "I never would have dreamed that these people were a part of something like this," she said excitedly. "They are just so simple, and appear so innocent, that it's hard for me to believe," stated Maggie.

"Well, it's the truth, Maggie," I told her, "that picture of the great granddaddy is Ali all over again. Just wait until you see it, they are so alike it's uncanny."

"Guy's going to make trouble for Ali and Viola, isn't he?" she asked, with a deep frown on her pretty face.

"Well, I think that I had better work something out with them," I said. "The worse the law can do to Ali right now is to deport him back to Mexico. But say they catch him with any of that gold, they are going to charge him as an accessory to robbery and murder. And even if it has been four generations away. Those FBI fellows will still charge anybody they possibly can. And to my knowledge, Guy is the only one who has enough memory of this past history to be able to stir up the shit for anyone.

"Well, Maggie, I am going to head for work now. Why don't you ask Aunt Betsey if she remembers anything about the Black Betsey. And the fact that old Adrian Recinos used her namesake as a title for his roadhouse."

"She will remember, all right," laughed Maggie. "The name is probably the reason that she never mentioned it to us."

I smiled in agreement. "Sounds like her, all right," I commented.

I took the Mexicans down to Running Springs that day. It's a small settlement southeast of Big Bear City, on the road to San Bernardino. We had lawn and brush cutting to do. A lot of it. Ali got the other five men started on various cutting and trimming projects.

"Ali," I said, "let's you and I take a little walk down by the springs. I want to talk with you in private."

Ali gave me a very concerned, if not, a bit worried expression. "What's up boss?" he asked me. "Me talk with you about anything."

"Okay, comrade," I said, and gave him a reassuring smile. I sat down at the picnic table next to the natural springs and motioned for Ali to sit across from me. I slowly and patiently laid the story onto him that Guy had related to me earlier that morning.

His expression was first, one of shocked surprise that I had become aware of this 90-year-old piece of past history, and that it involved his ancestors. Next his expression showed signs of possible flight.

"Just take it easy, Ali," I told him quietly, "I'm on your side."

And I explained to him what his position would be if the FBI even thought he was here in regards to retrieving the gold. Also I made sure that he realized where Guy stood. And that Guy was a very determined man, who would probably make trouble for Ali and his family, if he wasn't given some of the gold, with which to buy his silence. I continued, "As far as I am concerned, Ali, I have no idea, if you do or if you don't know anything about the whereabouts of this gold bullion. But I just want you to remember that Guy won't keep quiet for too long. So I am going to go now. I want you to think it over and I will be back to have lunch with you. So you can figure out what you want to tell me then."

"Yes, boss, yes, boss," he replied. His expression now one

of great concern and worry for himself and his family. I headed back to Big Bear City. I had work to do.

I took a bucket of Kentucky Fried Chicken back to Running Springs with me. I got Ali away from his comrades, and back to the picnic table beside the springs. We began to devour Colonel Sanders' best. Ali wore an expression of great relief. I could see that he had indeed made a decision.

"I'm going to tell all, boss," he said in his broken English. "You good man, boss, I trust in you. And know that you won't make harm for family, or me, Ali."

"No, Ali," I assured him, "I most certainly wouldn't do that."

"I do know where gold is. But I don't know where gold is. If you will help me, boss, you and that man Guy will help, then I think we can find gold. If we find gold, boss, you promise to me. I take half of all gold. You and Guy keep other half, okay?" he asked.

"I think that will work out just fine, Ali," I assured him. "That should be just fine."

"You see," he went on, "my grandfather knew where gold is. My father knew where gold is, but they couldn't find, FBI watch always. Watch always my grandfather. Watch always my father, they could not take chance to search. But now I don't think they watch, it has been long time they forget gold robbery, I watch very closely, but never see man watch me."

"I think you're right, Ali," I told him. "That's why it's so important to keep Guy quiet, he is the only one who still remembers. And if you hadn't have looked so much like your father and your great-grandfather, he wouldn't have remembered it either."

"That right, boss, that right, boss. Oh, I am so happy that you are my partners. It would have been difficult with me only. I was afraid when you mentioned it, but now feel only happy."

"I'm glad to have you for a partner too, Ali," I assured him. "We will make sure that everything works out."

"Come see me tonight after dark," said Ali in almost a whisper, "we take drive, I show."

After dropping the Mexicans off at their pickup truck that night, I took a drive over to the Crazy Horse. It was early evening and the place was almost deserted. Guy met me with a smile a mile wide. "Did you talk to him, Ter? Did you talk to the Mex?"

"Yes, Guy," I told him, "I sure did, let's you and I go into the private office for a minute or two. I don't want anybody to get even a sniff of what I'm about to tell you. I talked to Ali, and he is here for the gold," I told him.

"I knew it, I knew it, I knew that smart little replica of his great granddaddy was here for it," shouted Guy, in great excitement.

"Not so loud, Guy," I cautioned. "Some times even the walls have ears.

"Yes, he admitted to everything," I went on. "And being as he trusts me he made us a very generous offer. He's offering us half of the bullion in return for our silence. And our help in retrieving this fortune from its 90-year grave."

"Well, yes," said Guy, "the offer is more than fair. But what the hell chances are we going to have to take to retrieve it?" he asked, now with great excitement on his face.

"I don't know," I told him honestly. "But you be ready to drive at 9 p.m. tonight. I'm coming to pick you up. The Mex is going to take us out and show us where the treasure is at, and we will know then."

"Okay," said Guy, grinning from ear to ear. "There wouldn't be any chance of this little replica double crossing us would there be, Ter?" he asked suspiciously.

"Not a chance in hell," I assured him. "The little replica, as you call him, is only too glad to have us for partners." We shared a laugh and I left with a "I'll see you at nine."

I went home to share some of this exciting wealth of information with Maggie. Who had had a premonition that I was on my way home. And was barbecuing some delicious looking beefalo steaks. As I related this information to her, I could tell by the expression on her beautiful face. That she was fast becoming mesmerized by this piece of Big Bear Mountains exciting history.

"When I go to pick Ali up," I suggested, "why don't you grab a bottle of wine and go visit with Viola until we get back. As I am sure she would probably appreciate your company tonight, with all of this crap coming down. She will probably be in the need of some reassuring, just as Ali was."

"I was thinking that I would like to do that," came her pleasant reply. "But I didn't want to seem too much in the way of all of these other things."

"Don't you worry, Maggie, you will never be in the way," I assured her.

Ali and I headed for the Lincoln, leaving Viola and Maggie behind in deep, serious conversation, and a bottle of California white to spice up their evening. We pulled into the Crazy Horse parking lot. Guy was already and waiting for us outside the open door. I could hear Dean Martin's crooning voice coming off the jukebox. He was giving us, "That's Amore."

Guy jumped into the back seat of the Lincoln. And this time, instead of greeting Ali with a cold look and "I know your face from somewhere, mister," it was a firm handshake and, "How you doing, partner?"

Ali seemed overjoyed with this new approach. He shook Guy's hand like a pump handle, and repeated three times, "How you doing, partner."

We all laughed and went on our way.

Ali directed us onto the south road out of town. The road to San Bernardino. The same road that the Wells Fargo armored wagon had taken on that fateful day, over 90 years ago.

"Measure 2 miles on your car clock," said Ali, "then stop and I tell my partners what I know."

Two miles clicked by on the Lincoln's odometer. I pulled into a turn out on our right and stopped. Guy and I were now all ears as Ali started his fascinating story of so many years ago.

"It's somewhere near to us now, the gold is near, listen I tell." And his fascinating tale began…

"You see Great-Grandfather was a very wise and smart man. He knew gold was being sent in wagon that day. So he figure good plan to steal, and he steal all by himself. Nobody help. Great-Grandfather come here the night before wagon come. There be no horse or people on road. It be two, maybe three o'clock in morning. Road narrow then, just gravel and single file.

"Great-Grandfather has great plan. The moon makes road light. Great-Grandfather has pick, has shovel, digs great hole in exactly middle of road. Hole six feet deep, four feet round. Great-Grandfather has bucket, he carried dirt and gravel from hole to trees. He work real hard in moonlight. Great-Grandfather now has boards, six feet long. He lays boards over hole, digging them down a two inches, to be below top of road. Great-Grandfather now put 12 sticks of dynamite on top of boards. He run dynamite wires to trees. He take bucket and cover over boards and dynamite with thin layer of dirt and gravel. Great-Grandfather knew dynamite. He knew if you don't tamp it, it will blow up instead of down. To tamp means to cover dynamite with a heavy weight, which will then make blow down. Great-Grandfather knew that with just a sprinkle of gravel over the dynamite, it would blow its power up.

"Great-Grandfather go into trees with detonator box. Great-

Grandfather lay down and only sleep little bit. Morning come, Great-Grandfather see through trees. He sees armored wagon go by, going to refinery. Great-Grandfather wait two hours, he can hear wagon coming back. Great-Grandfather is ready with wires attached to detonating box. Wagon gets closer, horses pass on each side of dynamite. Wagon now on top of dynamite. Great-Grandfather pull on detonator. BOOM!!! Horse hitch blow off, horses run away. Dynamite blow up and take floor from wagon and break boards under dynamite. Big bunch of gold bars fall from wagon into bottom of big hole.

"Great-Grandfather now work real hard. He carry dirt back from trees in bucket. He fill hole to one foot from top of road, to make look like dynamite blow out one foot of earth. He make all rough. He gets cedar branch, he brush out all of his foot marks. Then Great-Grandfather rides horse all around wagon, making lots of horse feet. He now get second horse from trees, he ride that horse all around wagon too, making different horse feet. He now get third horse from trees, he make more horse feet with third horse. Then Great-Grandfather ride one horse and lead two, galloping south down the road for maybe one half-mile. He pulls off road and up into rocky area where he leave no horse feet. He stays with rocky area and cuts across country back to roadhouse.

"Everything would have been perfectly good with Great-Grandfather but dynamite blast wake up sleeping trapper. Trapper get up, look around, he recognize Great-Grandfather from a distance. Great-Grandfather's lawyer prove in court, trapper's eyes bad, couldn't see good far away. No gold was found, so no evidence to convict Great-Grandfather. Great-Grandfather could not go near gold. FBI watch for ten years. My grandfather could not go near gold FBI watch for years. My father they also watch. And when they change road and put pavement over gravel, Father give up and go back to Mexico.

"When I grow up Father tells me about his place Big Bear,

and he tells me about gold robbery. He tells me about road changing. Much wider and straighter. With pavement over gravel, and lots of cars coming and going. We real poor in Mexico, we always hungry. I get idea and so I come to Big Bear."

"What a story, Ali," I said, "that's a real fascinating story."

"It sure as hell is," agreed Guy from the back seat. He asked, "What is your plan, partner? Just how do you plan to retrieve that gold, now that we know it's six or seven feet below the pavement, on a real busy American highway."

"I think long time," answered Ali, "I figure there be only one way possible. I come here I work for Terry. I save money. I buy old truck, I go down to San Bernardino. I go army surplus store. I buy for one hundred dollars army mine detector. I come here often after midnight. I search highway with mine detector. When car come I run to ditch. Best at three o'clock in morning, no cars. I keep trying until one night mine detector go, beep, beep. I then mark spot with red paint. Also I mark edge of pavement with red paint. Then I come at nights and start tunnel from ditch to gold."

"You know," said Guy with enthusiasm, "that is like you say, Ali, the only sensible way that it could possibly be done."

"Yes," I agreed. "That is an ingenious plan. And about the only one I would be able to come up with myself."

Ali was now grinning from ear to ear, with his crude but practical plan being so readily accepted. And praised to boot.

I went down to Los Angeles the next weekend and purchased three twin box metal detectors. They were made by Whites Detector Company, and were designed to find large objects only, at depths up to 25 feet. They were top of the line and cost me twenty-five hundred for the three. The cost wasn't bothering me as long as I knew I had the right tool for the job. I presented Ali with this new machine. And much to his great delight, taught him to use it in the field up behind the Black Betsey. I explained to him that his army surplus army detector was only good for a short distance underground. And that he had possibly already passed over the gold without knowing it.

The three of us would now go out to the area, where we knew the gold was close to. And search the highway from 3 a.m. until 5 a.m. at least two mornings a week. We had been doing this for approximately two months now, and summer was gone. As a matter of fact, it was now late fall.

We were halfway through November, and no gold signs had been detected. I could see that Guy was getting very impatient. But he wasn't exactly complaining yet. Two weeks later, I informed all of my employees that it was all over for year 1987. And that I would be heading back down to the desert for the months of December, January, and February.

I asked Guy if he could give Ali enough work around the saloon for the next three months, to keep them in grocery money.

"He's a good cook," I told Guy, "and he could soon learn to sling beer."

Guy readily agreed to this arrangement. And much to my surprise he said, "You know, Ter, I have kind of got to like the little replica."

"That's good, Guy," I said. "One thing I know for sure, he sure won't cause you any problems."

"No," said Guy, "that's the way that I feel about him too. And I think that we should just shut down the highway hunting until you get back. I god damned near froze out there last night," he confessed.

"Of course, Guy," I agreed, "we know that it is out there somewhere. Let's just leave it for the warm weather."

CHAPTER FOURTEEN

BACK TO THE DESERT

Aunt Betsey was looking pretty down in the mouth when we said our goodbyes. She had gotten used to having us around. We left the motor home right where it sat. I made sure the plumbing was all drained, and checked the antifreeze in the radiator. We promised Auntie we would be back for Christmas Day. Then we climbed into the Lincoln and were on our way.

As we came around the corner that gave us our first glimpse of the old Black Betsey, Maggie said, "I want to stop and say goodbye to Viola."

"Yes, okay, Maggie," I said. "I was going to do that anyway."

The old roadhouse now bragged a big wood fired cookstove, in the middle of the main room, which had a roaring fire burning in its chambers. And was doing a good job of heating the place. In spite of the cracks in the walls, and the heavy construction plastic that covered the broken windows, in place of glass. Two large teakettles steamed away on its surface, creating a real homey effect. All 18 residents were inside the house today, as it was getting very cold outside, created by a strong north wind that howled around the outside walls of the notorious old Black Betsey.

"I'm leaving my chainsaw with you, Ali," I told him. "You will never keep this fire alive with that old buck saw that you have been using all fall."

"Thanks, boss," was his reply, "you save life of us all."

"There's five gallons of mixed gas there too, should last you awhile. When you mix the next can, just take it into the Texaco and tell them 25 to one."

"Okay, Terry, I remember." He smiled.

We could tell by the Mexicans' sad expressions as we said our goodbyes, just how much we had come to mean to these people. In the way of friendship and moral support, we assured them that we would stop and see them at Christmas time. And in the meantime, cut lots of wood and keep warm.

Our descent down Big Bear Mountain's east pass went smooth as silk. And we were in Desert Hot Springs before we knew it.

We stopped off to see Fat Billy. He was living in a cottage type house in the south end of town. I had a hard time visualizing how they could all fit in there. Fat Billy was in a joyous mood to see us. The cottage was a bedlam of screaming and crying children. Sylvia could be heard above the commotion.

"Billy, get milk. Billy, get diapers."

Billy stepped out on the porch and closed the door behind him. "Too damned noisy in there to even talk," he laughed. "What are you guys up to? Are you down for the winter?"

"Yes, we are," I told him. "It was getting a little too cold in Big Bear for camping out in the motor home. And as you know, the contracting business will be dead until next March."

"The weather is just beautiful here," Maggie said.

"Yes," said Billy, "I have a couple of roofing jobs that I have got to look at today."

I laughed openly. "How has the roofing business been this year, Billy?"

"Just as good as I want to make it," he laughed back. "You guys going back to Cathedral City?" he asked.

"No," I said, "the house that we lived in on Elvis Presley Boulevard has been leased out to somebody."

"Well, the reason that I asked," said Billy, "is that there is a nice two-bedroom for rent up on the hill behind the hot springs. There's a big sign out front, for sale or rent. You can't miss it, just go up on Fifty-first."

"Okay, Bill," I said, "we should look into it right away."

"Okay, Ter," said Bill. "Could you lend me a twenty? I have to buy gas for the truck so I can get to work."

"Sure, Bill," I said. I fished him a twenty out of my pocket. "Anything to keep you working," I added. We all enjoyed a laugh now. And then we went on our way, house hunting.

The house that Billy had suggested to us turned out to be a winner. It gave us a view of Desert Hot Springs, and of the entire surrounding valley. Also there was a small mountain formed from over thousands of years of shifting sand dunes. That I picked as an ideal place for my early morning jogging session, which I seldom ever missed doing. Even the rent was reasonable. And so we leased it for the next three months.

The following morning we were up with the sunrise, and anxious to try out our new jogging route. It was five blocks from our house to the bottom of this steep hill. With the blacktop road going straight up to the top and continuing to snake around the entire hill. Passing mansion, after mansion, of residential houses. Then it came back down the other side of the hill. I would judge the entire distance would be close to two and one half miles. With the steep hill making up a third of the distance. It was a tailor made to order running track. Which we both enjoyed each and every morning, through out the winter of 1987.

After showering and changing, following our brisk run. We decided to enjoy our toast and eggs, along with pan fries, out on the front porch. As we were finishing up our breakfast, the next door neighbors came over to introduce themselves. And to invite us over for an early morning swim in their back yard swimming pool. Their names were Paul and Sarah. They were in their mid sixties and seemed genuinely friendly. As they approached us from their yard, a half dozen roadrunners ran along with them. To me they had always been a comical looking bird. Reminding me so much of the movie cartoon character.

"Quite the little gathering of friends you have there," said Maggie, laughingly.

"Yes," said old Paul, "these guys are a must up here in this part of the desert. Are you new to the desert?" he asked us.

"Yes, you could say that," I answered. "We spent last winter in Cathedral City, but I don't have any history on the roadrunners," I told him frankly.

"Well, I'm glad to tell you about them," said old Paul, now very serious. "Whether you know it or not, we have a large population of snakes in these parts. There is the red racer, that reaches a length of 5 feet, but not venomous. Then we got the sidewinder, and he is a very poisonous rattler. Also the diamondback that grows up to 6 or 7 feet long, also venomous and dangerous, but most of them only come out at night when it is cool. You see, a couple of hours in the direct sunlight, will kill them. And so they stay hidden in holes in the ground or under rock piles, even under sheds and houses, if they can get in. And the point I'm making with you," he added, "is that these roadrunners are by far, the superior warriors. And run all the snakes off. All you've got to do is feed them a few scraps once or twice a day, and pretty soon you will have adopted 5 or 6 good snake guards."

"That is real interesting, Paul," I told him, "and I do thank you for the free knowledge. I really am not good with snakes at all," I added. "They have always left me with fear of contact. And I am definitely going to treasure these little characters from now on," I said, as I gestured towards the roadrunners. Which were now perched on the railing of our patio. And were looking us over with a quizzical eye.

We got into our swimsuits. Got a chilled bottle of California white wine, and went over to join Paul and Sarah at their little pool party. Now Maggie is one hell of a sight, in that little white bikini of hers. I would say a ten plus in sex appeal. Right from the beginning old Paul was agape with his mouth wide open. *The poor old guy is still horny, and Sarah has forgotten about it a long time ago*, I surmised to myself with humor. Our bottle of California white was now two thirds gone. And old Paul now had his patio chair smack up against Maggie's. And was trying to conduct a strictly one-on-one conversation. With nervous glances in my direction to see how I was taking it. I pretended I didn't see anything, as I have a good sense of humor. And know how capable Maggie is in taking care of herself.

Old Sarah was telling me all about the "vinegar spiders." They were a giant desert spider that stood 6 to 8 inches tall. They came out at night, traveling in great numbers in a marching army fashion. And little did she or I know that the laugh of the day was just about to happen.

By this time old Paul was leaning in Maggie's direction. And was practically whispering to her, with his face two inches from hers. Maggie spoke very loudly now, and glanced in my direction.

"My glass is empty, Paul, I need another cool drink," she said in a honey drip voice.

Now old Paul, half drunk on wine, and the other half drunk on Maggie, was so willing and eager to please this little dish.

And forgetting himself completely, jumped out of his patio chair like a twenty-year-old. The first thing that met our eyes was the projection in his swim trunks that was pushing the material 8 or 9 inches away from his body. He was reaching for the wine bottle in the ice container with his right hand when he too noticed this magical bulging in front of him. Immediately his left hand came down to conceal the bulge. This fast movement threw the old guy completely off balance. He now stumbled with his right hand on the California white, and his left hand over his erection. Into the pool went old Paul, bottle of wine and bottle cooler full of ice.

Now I don't know when I have had a better laugh, it came from my big toes right up to my ears. Maggie was practically in stitches. She was rocking back and forth with laughter in that old patio chair. And every time she looked at old Paul, it seemed to begin all over again. Old Paul by this time had overcome his momentary shock of surprise. He looked at us with an expression of shame and embarrassment. He reminded me of a dog coming home to a whipping. He climbed slowly out of the pool. The first thing that we noticed was that big bulge in front of his swim trunks had miraculously disappeared. This started us to laughing again. Old Paul now slunk past us with his tail between his legs. Muttering something about going in to use the john.

Maggie and I bid the also embarrassed Sarah goodbye. I didn't try to retrieve the bottle of wine, or the bottle cooler container from the bottom of the pool. As I stated to Maggie later, we should leave it in the pool to remind the old guy of the Tenth Commandment. "Thou shalt not convent thy neighbor's wife." This started us to laughing all over again. This time we really laughed ourselves out, it had been quite a day. We didn't see Paul for quite a spell after our first pool party. He now seemed to be a homebody.

CHAPTER FIFTEEN

MR. DIAMONDBACK

The story that Paul had told us, in regards to a large snake population, was to leave me without a doubt, as to the authenticity of his story.

"This little experience, I wish to share with you."

It all started with Fat Billy the Roofer. He and Sylvia's wedding anniversary had rolled around. I belief it was their eighth. Anyway, it seemed that the pickins in the roofing racket had been good to Billy. He had taken it upon himself to rent the banquet room in Jeannie's Bar. Which was located on the main street of Desert Hot Springs. As he stated to me with a grin, "A fellow has to show his woman that she is appreciated."

Billy was wearing his wedding tux. He looked charming, right down to the blubber hanging over his belt sash. Sylvia looked good also. Her wedding gown still fitted her well, in spite of 7 children. She had arrived complete with the two youngest babies, who were now sleeping in cribs on top of the bar. There were four other couples present, friends of Bill's, and completely unknown to Maggie and I. Billy had brought his record collection. He liked the oldies as much as I did. And was now playing the old Guy Mitchell hit from 1950, "There's a Pawnshop Around the Corner in Pittsburgh Pennsylvania." This being Billy's hometown, we had kind of made it our theme song. I know that some of you out there do remember this song, and will appreciate the memory of it.

Anyway the party was a success. Everyone was in a good state of mind. Maggie and I had brought along a case of champagne, so Billy had the place supply us with, not one, but four, champagne bottle coolers. Every time I looked at one of those bottle coolers, I would think of old Paul taking his unexpected dive into the pool, accompanied by the bottle cooler. So great was the memory that I took it upon myself to relate the story to Billy and his guests, who enjoyed it immensely.

I checked my wrist clock, it was now three-thirty a.m., and the only party people left in the banquet room were Maggie and I, Bill and Sylvia and the two babies. We dropped the happy little family off at their cottage, then headed for our own house on Fifty-first Avenue. It was 4 a.m., and I think now, that the champagne had impaired my judgement a bit. As we alighted from the car I suddenly got this bright idea. I said, "Maggie, it's just about morning already. And I was just thinking that we should go for our run up the mountain and back now instead of at sun up. This way we can get to sleep in, and still have not missed our daily exercise."

Maggie shrugged my idea off as kind of bizarre. She informed me to suit myself, but she was going to bed now. Not to spoil a good idea, I got on the sweatshirt, shorts and running shoes, and was on my way in the direction of the mountain. I remember starting my run up this steep incline. Also I remember that my legs were feeling champagne weak. At about the halfway mark I decided to sit down for a moment, to get the strength back in my legs.

I sat down in the ditch and leaned back on the sand, which

still held much of yesterday's heat. In this comfortable position, I was soon in a deep slumber. I guess I slept for approximately 2 hours. I awoke with the warm rays of the rising sun on my face. My first impulse was to jump up and stretch as I always do in the morning. Now what I am about to tell you, happened in seconds, not minutes, as it seemed at the time.

I first became aware of a foul smelling stench. And at the same instance I also became aware of an unfamiliar weight on my chest. Squinting my eyes against the rising sun, I glanced down at my chest, and looked smack into the face of a "diamondback rattler." Now this guy was big. He was coiled on my chest with its head pointing towards my face. It also was asleep, the eyes were closed. In spite of my party haze of the night before, I now became damned cautious. My first impulse was to grab it by the neck and try to throw it away from me. This idea I immediately discarded. As I decided that my chances of actually grabbing this monster, which was 5 to 6 feet long and being able to hurl it away from me before it struck and bit me, was one in a million. *What to do??? What to do???* was going through my desperate mind. The stench now seemed to be getting stronger. I realized he had crawled on me and coiled up to absorb my body heat. As the nights are cold on the desert. My feverish mind now had a plan that I was acting out as fast as it came to me. I dug my heels into the sand. Slowly bending my knees up a few inches. I put all of my upper body weight on my elbows. *Make it damned good*, I remember this thought going into the plan. And I did. I gave one tremendous flip of my midsection towards the clear blue sky. Mr. Diamondback went straight up in the air. The split second that his weight left my chest, I had rolled to the left three times, before he hit the sand where I had made my bed last night. The big snake, being awakened so abruptly, was gone in a flash. I watched him with eyes of relief, as he slithered into the mesquite brush that clung to the hillside.

Now I did stretch, and continued my run up the mountainside. Counting my blessings that I wasn't dead. Or in some hospital, recovering from rattlesnake venom. And knowing full well that Maggie's idea of a few hours ago had truly been the answer. I also remembered old Paul's words: "There is quite a population of snakes in this part of the desert."

Maggie and I stayed in bed that day until high noon. And were now enjoying our brunch on the front porch, with our pet roadrunners, who now amounted to eight. They were a comical, likeable little creature, they would try to correspond with us through verbal conversation. Squawking and cocking their heads this way and that way, and jumping up on our knees, if we didn't try to correspond back to them.

I asked old Paul one day, "What's going to become of these little guys when we move on?"

"Oh," he said, matter-of-factly, "don't be concerned about these guys, they just move on to the next stranger who hasn't already got some. I kind of think that they know that this is their job on the desert, and they just go ahead with life."

I thanked old Paul, and told him that nobody could have answered my question more thoroughly then he just had.

It was December 24th in Desert Hot Springs. Maggie was bustling around the house, getting all the Christmas necessities ready for Big Bear City. Fat Billy and I were enjoying a cup of coffee out on the front porch. He had came to see me that morning for two reasons. Number one being. A friend of his was doing some renovating on the Gene Autry Hotel in Palm Springs, and was desperately in need of a good bricklayer, to construct a large chimney on the outside wall of the building. We reached this guy by telephone and made arrangements to meet with him there, on the first working day after New Year's. The second reason being, that it was in fact Christmas Eve and

Fat Billy needed some money. I was able to lend him $500 without going short in anyway myself. And so he went on his way with a hearty "Merry Christmas and a Happy New Year," and a smile as wide as Desert Hot Springs.

CHAPTER SIXTEEN

ALI DISAPPEARS

We had decided to head out for Big Bear City on the morning of the 25th. And were in fact on our way out of Desert Hot Springs at six-thirty a.m. The weather and the road conditions were excellent, which reminded me of the racehorse track announcement that they used to broadcast before a race started. This was when I was living in Calgary, it went like this, "The sky is clear and the track is fast." Before we knew it we were cruising through Lucerne Valley, and then starting our ascent of Big Bear Mountain. The climb went as smooth as silk. Maggie and I remembering our trip up here in the motor home, and the abuse that we had got thrown our way at the top of the summit. We shared a hearty laugh in memory.

We were now over the hump and starting down the other side. "We should soon be able to see Viola and Ali's chimney smoke," I said to Maggie, "it's damned cold up here."

"I was thinking the same thing," said Maggie, with a puzzled expression on her pretty face. And we soon found out why there was no smoke. As we came abreast of the old Black Betsey, we could see that it was deserted. Being as the snow in the driveway was too deep to drive in, we parked on the shoulder.

"I think we better get in there and see what the hell is going on, don't you, Maggie?" I asked.

"We sure better," was her quiet answer. I broke trail up to the notorious old roadhouse, the snow was a good 10 to 12 inches deep up here. We made the porch, I tried the front door and found it locked up tight.

"I'll go around back and check the back door," I said. I circled the quiet building and found the back door unlocked. I left the door open to let in the sunlight, as it was dark and dingy in there with no window glass. I walked straight through to the front door and let Maggie in.

"What's happening?" she asked, with a questioning look on her face.

"I don't know," I muttered, "it looks like they all just walked out."

All the furnishings still remained as we remembered. Right down to my chain saw, which was sitting behind the huge wood stove, on a pile of wood. "Better take this," I said, and set the saw out on the front porch. We went over the place in detail, hoping for a clue. Or possibly a letter of explanation, but found nothing.

Next stop was Aunt Betsy's, who was overjoyed to have us, on this Christmas Day on Big Bear Mountain, year 1987. I left Maggie with Auntie. And being as it was past high noon, I took a drive down to the Crazy Horse to see if I could get some word on what had happened to Ali and his gang. Guy had closed the bar for the day. So I knocked on the side door, which opened immediately.

"Saw you pulling in," said Guy. "How's it going, Ter?" was his greeting.

"Things are always good with me, Guy," I told him with a big smile. "What the hell happened to Ali and his followers?

Maggie and I stopped up there and checked the place out, looks like they just walked out."

"Well, I really don't know for sure," said Guy with that suspicious look on his face. "But as far as I'm concerned there is only two possible answers to your question. Ali did work here for a while, and got to be a damned good beer slinger. About a month after you left, he didn't show up for evening shift, and hasn't been seen since. But like I say, Ter," said Guy, lighting up a smoke, "there is only two possible answers as to what happened to him."

"I'm listening, go on," I said.

"Well, I have been doing a lot of thinking about that little replica. Now there is a chance that the immigration caught up with them, and deported them back to Mexico. Then there is the chance that the little bastard actually got to the gold and shipped out with it."

"What's your hunch, Guy?" I asked him, already knowing what his answer would be. Guy had that suspicious expression on his face again.

"My hunch says that little replica not only hoodwinked both of us, but double crossed us in the name of a friend."

"I hope it's not that way, Guy," I stated evenly. But even as I answered him, I kind of had the feeling that he was right.

"Do you know anybody down in San Bernardino who could check the immigration records for us?" I asked.

"No," said Guy, "but better than that, I will get our own chief of police of Big Bear to find out for us on Monday. He went to school with the little replica's father and I. And if they haven't been deported, then we will know for sure that we have been played for the fool." Little did either of us know that we were soon to find out anyway. In a different sort of way.

I bid Guy a Merry Christmas, and we shared a drink of brandy. "I have to go back in the morning," I told him. "Jot down my number in Desert Hot Springs and let me know the results of the immigration question as soon as you find out."

"I sure will," said Guy, "and enjoy your Christmas," he added.

We had enjoyed an excellent Christmas dinner with Aunt Betsey. And were settling down to watch the Robert Mitchum movie that I had given to Auntie as a Christmas present. It was entitled *Cape Fear*, being the first version of this tense drama. It starred Aunt Betsy's Robert Mitchum, along with Gregory Peck. I could see that the movie was the best thing that I could have possibly given the old girl. She definitely had a twinkle in her eye as she watched these two young and handsome actors. From the beautiful colorful era of the 1950s.

Boxing Day found us on our way back to Desert Hot Springs. Both Maggie and I felt a deep sadness. And also a bit of disappointment, as we passed thc now deserted Black Betsey. Which looked alone and forlorn, as it peered out at us from under its veil of snow.

It was now Monday morning. Maggie and I were enjoying a cup of coffee out on our front porch on Fifty-first Avenue. The roadrunners had also gathered for breakfast. And were telling us some kind of a story, but in their own lingo, mind you. My cell phone rang.

"Who do you say that is, Maggie?" I asked her.

"Well, I don't think that it is Fat Billy," she mused. "You had better answer it, because I really don't know this time."

"Hello." She was right, it wasn't Fat Billy. It was Guy's voice booming over the wires from Big Bear.

"Hello yourself," he roared, "just called to tell you that little replica didn't get deported. There's been no one deported out of this area for over two years," he added. "This is quite a kick in the ass," he went on. "You know what $300,000 worth of gold in 1898 would be worth now, don't you?"

"Not off hand, Guy," I answered, "but I do know it's worth one hell of a lot more now."

"I figured it out, Ter," he continued, "and that pile of bullion is now worth 18 million American dollars. That would have been four and one half million apiece, that it looks like we have just got screwed out of."

"That's mighty big numbers, Guy," I answered. "Maybe there is still hope for it," I said. But I really didn't believe it, even as I spoke the words.

"You guys coming up for New Year's?"

"No we won't be up now until March," I told him, "I have some work to do here, right after New Year's."

"Okay," said Guy. "I'll see you then."

"Yes and thanks for the information," I said.

"Okay," said Guy in a tired and kind of disappointed voice. "I'll let you know if anything else pops up."

"Okay, Guy, oh by the way, has anyone seen or heard from Morningstar?"

I saw Maggie's expression turn to worry lines when I asked this last question.

"Not a damned word, just like he disappeared right off the face of the earth," was his reply.

"What did he say about Mr. Morningstar?" asked Maggie when I had hung up.

"Nobody has seen or heard anything about Donnie," I answered her. "And don't you punish yourself about it, Maggie, we thought that we were doing him a kindness. You didn't mean it to turn out this way. And anyway, maybe he is perfectly all right, where ever he is," I added. But I could see that my sense of reasoning wasn't really doing that much good.

It was now New Year's Eve in Desert Hot Springs. Old Paul and Sarah had stopped in for one drink. And wished us the best of the season. It had now been one drink only, with the neighbors since Paul's pool party, and his unexpected dive into the swimming pool. I would bet my bankroll on Sarah being the instigator of this. Anyway it was definitely the answer, as old Paul with only one drink was a perfect gentleman. Paul and Sarah had left and Maggie reminded me that it was time to go pick up Bill and Sylvia. Just at that moment my cell phone rang.

"Must be Billy getting impatient," I said, as I picked up the phone.

I was just about to say hi Billy, when Guy's loud voice boomed across the wires from Big Bear Mountain. There was no preliminary greetings of any kind, like hello, or is that you? Instead, he was shouting.

"Now we know. Now we know for god damned sure, Ter. That god damned little Mexican replica son-of-a-bitch done it. The little bean eating Mexican son-of-a-bitch actually done it. I'll be god damned if he didn't." I could tell by Maggie's expression that she could hear every word that Guy was shouting, from where she sat, ten feet away from the phone. Which I was holding 6 inches away from my ear, so as not to lose an eardrum.

"Slow down, Guy," I said, "slow down and tell me what happened."

His volume dropped only an octave or two. "Wait till you hear this," he went on. "About noon today, a tractor-trailer, bound for San Bernardino, broke through the pavement 3 miles south of Big Bear City. The rear wheels of the trailer were caught in a hole in the pavement and pulled them completely off the trailer. They had the whole god damned highway shut down for hours. Just one hell of a time. People couldn't get in here and nobody could get out. The god damned traffic was backed up away past the Crazy Horse and then some. And you know what, Ter? The repair crew, who were the first on the scene, stopped in here for a beer on their way home. And do you know what they told me?" Guy was shouting again.

"Yes, Guy," I said. "Slow down, I want to know. What did they tell you?"

"They told me that someone had dug a god damned mystery tunnel under the highway. All the way from the ditch on the low side, to 4 feet past the white line in the middle. And you know what? That tunnel was all shored up real good, with two-by-fours and heavy plywood. The workmen figured that the frost heaves had loosened the supports and let it cave in. Can you imagine that little replica son-of-a-bitch. I gotta give him credit," shouted Guy. "I hate the little bastard, but I just gotta give him credit. Why the conniving little son-of-a-bitch. What the hell do you think we can do about it, Ter?"

And before I could answer. He went on, "That god damned conniving little bastard had us searching just two miles out of town. A whole god damned mile from where we should have been. You know I god damned near froze my buns off out there. And that little replica bastard was laughing all the time."

I just about had to laugh myself. As the value of the gold had never been an issue with me right from the beginning. But realizing how upset my friend had become. I comforted him with, "I'm certainly going to look into it, Guy. But there definitely won't be anything that we can do about it until after New Year's."

"Okay," Guy answered. Settling down a bit now. "But you had better come see me as soon as you can, will you promise?" he shouted. "We have to come up with a plan."

"Okay, Guy, don't tell anyone anything about the gold. I'll be up to see you on the weekend. Next Saturday."

This seemed to pacify him somewhat. He bade me "A Happy New Year's," and was gone.

"Oh my ear," I smiled at Maggie. "Did you hear all of that as well as I did?" I asked her.

"Just about every word," she stated. And then she added,

looking a little unsure of how I would take it, but having to say it anyway, "I'm glad that Ali got the gold and that they all got away. After all, it was his family who stole it in the first place. And another thing I'm sure of," she went on, "you will hear from Ali again. I know that he really liked you. And he is just not that kind of a man who would spit on his friends."

"You know what, Maggie?" I said very seriously now. "I'm glad that he got it too. It really didn't mean that much to me. The only reason that I was actually a part of it was to keep old Guy from spilling the beans and spoiling it for everyone. And yes I think you are a very good judge of character, Maggie. Ali definitely will contact us sometime in the near future."

We didn't know it for sure that day, "but he did."

CHAPTER SEVENTEEN

GOOD NIGHT IREENE

New Year's was a few laughs at home with Bill and Sylvia. They had hired an all-night babysitter, and so had slept over with us. When Maggie and I were getting ready, a little late, for our run up the mountain, Fat Billy was snoring like a freight train.

"How can Sylvia lie there and not wake up?" Maggie wondered out loud.

"It looks kind of difficult, all right," I agreed. "I guess we would have to put it down to familiarity. Or maybe Sylvia is aware of the old saying, 'Snoring is sweet music to a widow.'"

"I'll take the widow position any day," laughed Maggie. And somehow I just had to agree with her.

Monday morning came early. I went down to pick the fat man up as he was going into Palm Springs with me. He wanted to introduce me to his friend, who was doing the renovating at the Gene Autry Hotel. To my way of thinking he was going just because he was afraid of missing something.

This contractor, Albert, turned out to be a real likeable sort. And we made a deal on the chimney for $8,000. And I was going to get a start on it the following morning.

"Billy," I said, "as you know, my cube van is up on Big Bear Mountain. Would you be able to bring your pickup in here tomorrow morning and haul me in 10 sections of scaffolding? The bricks and mortar I can have delivered," I told him, "but I know that they won't deliver the scaffolding."

"Sure," said Billy. "I will pick you up in the morning. You don't even have to bring your Lincoln. I got some jobs to look at tomorrow in Rancho Mirage. I'll pick you up at 5 and give you a ride home also," he said, very pleased with himself for being able to be such a big help.

"Okay, Billy, I appreciate it," I told him, as I dropped him off at his cottage.

"Aren't you coming in?" he asked expectantly.

I could hear the kids screaming from the driveway and declined with. "Not this time, Billy. Maggie's got some errands for me to do today, we will have a beer after work tomorrow."

"You bet we will, Ter," he grinned and headed for the cottage.

Billy was as good as his word. He had me on the job by nine the next morning, and left to pick up the scaffolding. The first day on the job worked out just fine. I always work without a helper the first day, on this type of job. As there is nothing to be carried up the ladders. I was in fact, ten feet up the wall, with a ten-foot wide brick chimney, by the time Billy pulled in at 5 p.m. sharp.

"How did the roofing go today?" I asked, as we pulled out on the northbound lane, in the direction of Desert Hot Springs. Fat Billy didn't answer me verbally. Instead, he flipped open the beer cooler that was sitting on the floor of the truck cab, showing me that it was full of beer and ice. And then with his twelve-inch grin in place, dipped his hand into his jacket pocket and produced a handful of fifty- and twenty-dollar American bills. I just grinned back at him and opened a beer for us both.

We were now off the freeway and onto the two-lane blacktop that took us through the valley of sand dunes to Desert Hot Springs. Now Billy's sense of humor was a bit distorted at times, but I never paid much attention to the fact. I will now share a little example of what I mean with you.

We were cruising the two-lane at an approximately 50 or 60 miles per hour. We were singing our theme song, "There's a Pawnshop Round the Corner in Pittsburgh Pennsylvania." Billy now left the blacktop on our right, down through the ditch that was wide and sloping, up the other side, and then continued right up the steep sand dune that was now facing us. And having to gear down to do it. Much to my surprise, the old pickup flew over the summit, and started to quickly gain momentum as we flew down the other side, and back onto the blacktop, still at 50 or 60 miles per hour. Old Billy never offered any word of explanation for this little act, so I could see no reason to question him. I simply snapped open a couple of more beers. And we took another go at, "The Pawnshop in Pennsylvania."

We sat on my front porch and had a few more cool ones. Maggie, who I think was getting a little tired of, "The Pawnshop in Pittsburgh Pennsylvania," was telling me that I should shower up as supper was almost ready. Fat Billy got the message and bid me a hearty good night. He left in a cloud of sand and dust. Singing another one of Guy Mitchell's oldies, "One of the Roving Kind."

It was the third day on the job. I was now halfway up the second story. I would say I had built a good 16 feet of chimney. I had hired a real good Mexican helper for minimum wage. And things were rolling along first class.

But like I have suggested a few chapters back. My life always seems to be guided by these unseen forces, and I guess they were at work that day. I was, in fact, contentedly working away and singing our theme song, "There's a Pawnshop Round the Corner in Pittsburgh Pennsylvania," when I was hailed by a pleasant female voice.

"Hey, you over there, hey, bricklayer."

I turned in the direction of this pleasant voice. She was standing out on the balcony of her apartment. The apartment building being directly across the alley from the Gene Autry Hotel, where I was constructing this beautiful antique brick chimney. With her apartment being on the second floor, we were now directly in line with each other.

I noticed that she wasn't young anymore. I would say around 50. But she looked good. Quite tall for a woman from that era, I would judge her at five foot six or seven inches. Her body was good. And her hair was blonde and hung almost to her waist.

"Hey yourself," I said, and smiled at her.

"Where did you get that song from?" she asked.

"Oh, that," I laughed. "That's one of Guy Mitchell's hits from the early fifties."

"I know," she said, "my ex-husband used to sing it a long time ago."

"Yes, well it is catchy," I answered her.

"And you're from Canada, aren't you?" she said.

"Yes, I sure am," I replied.

"I want to see you," she said. "I have a business proposition for you. Are you married?" was her next question.

"No," I told her truthfully, "not for a long time."

"Good," she said, giving me a big smile. "I'm in 204, will you come over now?"

I looked at my wrist clock. It was already four-fifteen. "Yes," I said, "give me ten minutes."

"Okay," she replied pleasantly, and disappeared back inside.

The young Mex and I cleaned up the bricks, and put the tools away for the day. I paid him in cash for the day's labor and asked, "You come tomorrow?"

"Me come, me come happy," he stated, with a great smile of

white teeth. “Time nine?” he asked.

“Yes, time nine,” I grinned back at him.

“Maybe you don’t come at nine,” he joked, and pointed up at the blonde’s window. We both laughed and went our separate ways. I buzzed 204.

“Come on up, Canuck,” said the pleasant voice.

I was impressed with this lavish apartment of hers. It was spacious, and furnished with the finest that money could buy. I smelled money. Big money.

“Will you join me for a drink of California cider?” she asked.

“Yes,” I said, “over ice please.”

“That’s how I like it too,” she said, giving me a lush smile.

I took a seat at the large walnut table. She put down a mug of cider and ice in front of me. I took a large swig, sighed and said, “Well, that sure hits the spot.”

I could see that she was a little impatient, and wanted to get down to business.

“My name is Terry Fraser,” I said.

“I’m Ireene,” she said.

“What’s on your mind, Ireene?” I asked with genuine curiosity.

“You definitely are a Canadian citizen with papers to prove it?” she asked.

“Yes, born and raised,” I said. “And I do carry all Canadian ID.” I took out my wallet and produced all the necessary documents.

“And you are single?” she asked again as she looked over my ID.

“Yes,” I answered. “But I have no way of proving that.”

“That’s okay,” she said, “I believe you. You Canadians are very poor liars. I know, I used to have a boyfriend from Kelowna, B.C. He used to try to lie but he couldn’t. All right,” said Ireene, looking me over like she was buying a racehorse,

"I have to start somewhere. How about you and I getting married?" she asked, with a smile.

"Why would I want to do that?" I asked, a bit amused now.

"Well, I would say it would be for the money only, being as you barely know me," she answered.

"Yes, I suppose you're right," I laughed. "And why would you want to marry me?" I asked her.

"To save my ass," she stated flatly. "Listen up now and I will tell you the whole story. You see," she went on, "I was in business with my son. He is a Sagittarius, which makes him a died in the wool playboy and con man." *Maybe Fat Billy is a Sagittarius*, I thought to myself.

"Anyway to make a long story short. Jerry, my son, juggled the records and accounts to the point where the IRS wants to strip me of almost everything that I own. Jerry took his money and ran. Leaving me holding the bag."

She continued, "The IRS have suggested a figure close to $300,000. I have liquidated most of my assets, and now need a Canadian husband, which my lawyer tells me, will make it next to impossible to have me extradited from Canada."

"I don't have any idea how the law works in a case like that," I told her.

"You don't have to," she said. "My lawyer is the man who I am paying to do all of the thinking."

I was not quiet as slow a thinker as this troubled lady seemed to think. I realized that once married to her, I would be stuck with the marriage for life. Which I definitely didn't want. I knew that for her own protection, there was no way that she would agree to a divorce for many years. And I was thinking that possibly there was no statute of limitations, where the IRS was involved. But I was getting an idea, so I looked Ireene square in the eye and asked, "What kind of figure were you prepared to pay, for a good healthy Canadian husband?"

"I haven't even thought about that," she said.

I could tell by her expression that she was telling a barefaced lie. She had put lots of thought into it. But she had me figured to be dumb enough to maybe to do it for peanuts. She smiled at me sweetly now, and said in a honey drip voice, "What would you want from me to do a little favor like this, dear?" And at the same time she was starting to play footsies with me under the table.

I looked at her and jarred her out of her little romantic act with. "$20,000," I said. "Twenty thousand in American dollars, cash."

She was once more the businesswoman. And I will state, a much more cautious and not so friendly opponent. "Oh God, I can't afford that," she whaled, now appearing close to tears. "Oh God, why does everyone want to take all of my money?" she moaned.

Her act was good, but it was completely wasted on me as I could see clear through her. And I figured that if the IRS wanted $300,000, she would have to be worth close to a million.

"Okay, Ireene," I said pleasantly. "Suit yourself, I have to be on my way now."

"No, no, wait," she pleaded. "I did think about it and I'm prepared to pay $10,000."

I grinned at her and got up from the table. "No, Ireene," I answered evenly. "$10,000 only puts you halfway to the alter. Think it over tonight. I'll be right outside your window in the morning."

She looked at me with crocodile tears trickling down her cheeks. She swallowed, and then muttered, in a small defeated voice, "Okay, good night now." I closed the door and took the stairs down. I knew full well that the $20,000 was as good as mine. This lady was desperate. She had no idea how long before the IRS would be kicking her door down.

Upon reaching Desert Hot Springs, I pulled the Lincoln into

Fat Billy's driveway. Billy was on the porch in a recliner, sipping a can of Budweiser.

"You ever been a priest, Bill?" I asked him seriously.

He looked at me very inquisitively. "No," he stated flatly. And sensing that something was in the wind, he hurriedly added, "But I sure could be."

"That's what I thought," I said with a grin. I added, "If you can be a damned good one there is a thousand in it for you."

Now I was talking the fat man's language. He was wearing that ready to please smile, and kept repeating. "Tell me about it, Ter, tell me about it, Ter."

I ran the story past Billy. He was game; in fact, he was more than game. He now had a challenge that interested him, he was happy.

"Just one thing bothers me, Ter," he said, around his beer can.

"And what's that?" I asked.

"Well, what if this woman wants some verification as to my standing in the church?"

"Well, the way I see it Billy," I told him directly, "if you put on a convincing enough show, why should she ask or even be suspicious?"

"That's right, that's right," said Billy, brightening up now.

"Okay, what do you need?" I asked him.

"I'll need a Bible," he said. "A nice big Bible." I marked this down in my pad.

"Can you still get into your tux?" I asked him.

"No," he said, "I can't." I marked down, dark suit.

"Shoes?" I asked.

"Oh, I got shoes," he said.

"And how about a white collar and a black shirt?" I asked.

"We'll have to get that," he said. I marked them down too.

"Okay, Billy," I said, "you get your bums into Palm Springs first thing in the morning. Go to the secondhand store and make sure that you get all of this stuff. And get your speech, or sermon, or whatever you want to call it, prepared. And listen, we have to do this either tomorrow or the next day. Maggie will be back from Los Angeles Saturday morning, and I don't want her knowing anything about this. I'm going to have Ireene call you herself. So when you get back from Palm Springs with all of this stuff, go up to my house and sit tight until the phone rings. Got it all?" I asked him seriously.

"Cut and dried," he answered, "cut and dried."

I gave him $300 for the costume party. And the spare key to my house.

"And remember to answer the phone with, 'Church of Christ, Reverend William Mcphee speaking.'"

Bill scribbled this down, grinning very wide now.

I went down to the one-hour press and got the smallest amount of business cards that they would turn out, which was a minimum of 24 cards. I picked the most elaborate design that they had in their samples and ordered it as follows:

THE LOYAL CHURCH OF CHRIST FAITH
Reverend William J. Mcphee Presiding
In House Baptismals and Weddings
2020 51st Avenue, Desert Hot Springs
Phone 722-1414

The cards were of the highest quality. I was so impressed that I dropped by Billy's cottage and gave him half of them. He looked them over with a quizzical eye, and then said, with an air of importance, "Well done, my son."

Seeing that he was serious, I didn't comment on this surprise role that he was now exercising. But I begin to realize that this big lug was a born actor. And was already taking on the personality of, in fact, "a priest."

The little Mex and I were bricklaying in harmony the next morning. The job was going exceptionally well. It was ten-fifteen when the blonde made her appearance. I guessed that she was not an early riser.

"Hey you, Mr. Fraser," she called across the alley.

We were a bit above her balcony level now. I turned and looked down at her. "Good morning, Ireene," I answered.

"Come on over," she said. "Can you come right away? This is important."

"Okay," I called back. "Be there in five."

I left with the little Mexican mimicking me in his high-pitched voice, "Be there in five."

I gave him a dirty look, and a little shove as I went past. He now erupted with laughter. Ireene buzzed me in. She poured me a coffee and got right down to business. "I done a lot of thinking last night, Terry, and I think you are charging me too much for this. But I am prepared to pay it under one condition."

"And what's the condition, Ireene?" I asked her quietly.

"The condition is that we do this right away. I don't have time for any dragged out affair," she said, very abrupt now.

"Okay, okay," I said, "I'll tell you what, if you go down to the city hall right away, you can take my ID and get the California marriage license."

"And what about a priest?" she asked. "Sometimes people have to make an appointment a week or two down the road for a wedding."

"Not to worry," I told her. "I attend a church every Sunday in Desert Hot Springs and have gotten to know the presiding reverend very well. And I don't think that he's all that busy," I added. "As a matter of fact, I think that I have one of his business cards." I shuffled through my wallet. "Doesn't seem to be here." I pretended disappointment. "Where did I put that card? Where the hell did I put that card?" I said half to myself. "Oh," I jumped up, "it's in the glove box. Yes I remember now, just hold on, Ireene, I'll go down to the car and get it."

I returned and handed her the card. She looked it over

appreciatively. “Wow,” she said, “if we can get this done today I will be one happy woman.”

“Well,” I suggested, “why don’t you phone the reverend yourself and see when he can do this. Mention my name and tell him that we had decided to get hitched on the spur of the moment. And want to do it as soon as possible.”

Ireene, now smiling and filled with enthusiasm, dialed up Fat Billy. I could hear his voice from where I sat across the table from Ireene. They spoke briefly. Ireene giving him her number and put the phone down.

“What did the rev have to say?” I asked, matter-of-factly.

“Oh, he seems real nice,” she said with a smile. “He’s checking his appointment book, and will call us back pronto.”

It was all I could do to keep from bursting out in a fit of laughter. Billy had it all together, I didn’t have to worry about him. Ireene poured me another cup of coffee. Five minutes later the telephone rang. Ireene’s voice was now all honey.

“Yes, Reverend Mcphee, yes, Reverend, we will get the license this morning, can you, Reverend? Oh, that’s just beautiful, Mr. Mcphee. Yes, he’s here. I certainly will say hi to Mr. Fraser for you. Yes, Reverend, he has spoken very highly of you already. Okay, Reverend, three o’clock it is then. And what did you say the fee was? One hundred dollars. Okay that’s just fine, Reverend, see you at three. Yes, I’m sure Terry knows how to find your house,” she was saying.

I turned my head to hide a smile on that one. Ireene put down the phone, she was overjoyed.

“Finely,” she yelled, “finely things are working out. Yahooo!” she hollered, giving me a big bear hug. “Give me your damned ID I’m out of here,” she yelled gaily. We left together.

The little Mex and I watched as Ireene backed her Mercedes sports car out of the underground parking. She left with a wave and a smile as big as Palm Springs.

"Big money, boss," stated the Mexican, as he watched her disappear. "Big money, car cost plenty."

"Yes, Chico," I said, "that little car retails for $120,000 this year."

"Wow," said Chico, "wow, you going to get her, boss?" he asked excitedly.

"I think so," I said jokingly, "but just for a little while."

He eyed me like he had just met Rudolph Valentino. "Maybe you should keep, boss," he said very seriously.

"We will see, Chico," I told him. "But listen, I have something real important to do today. So I am giving you the rest of the day off. I'm real happy about things today," I went on. "So after you clean everything up real good, I will pay you for the full day. But stay sober and be here tomorrow morning."

Chico was now grinning from ear to ear. "I sober, boss, be here morning."

Suddenly I realized that I didn't own a suit and would have to get one pronto. I went down to the secondhand store and got a dandy tux, complete with a pleated shirt, for one hundred American. And a beautiful pair of black patent leather shoes for twenty-five. Ireene was home when I got back and buzzed me up. I used her shower and changed into the tux. It fitted me great. Even the shoes were comfortable and shone up beautifully.

When I stepped out of the bedroom, where I had been changing. Ireene said, "Wow, Terry, you wouldn't be too bad of a grab at all. As long as we could keep you out of those working togs of yours."

"Some of us got to do it, Ireene," I told her, "you're old enough to realize that."

"I'm old enough to realize a lot more than I do," she said gaily.

Ireene looked great. She was dressed in a white strapless

evening gown. Matching white shoes. And a white fur from some poor unfortunate animal, draped across her shoulders. She looked great. And I told her so. And much to my dismay, she gripped me around the neck and gave me a long and lingering kiss.

"Hope you didn't mind," she said in an apologetic voice. "But after all, it is my wedding day."

"That's all right," I assured her. "I guess it's my wedding day too."

We decided to enjoy a drink of cider, and so sat down at the walnut table. I could see that Ireene was getting all lovey and romantic. And I began to realize that women would be moved in a situation like this, where a man wouldn't.

"Well, it's two-fifteen," she said, "don't you think that we had better be on our way?"

"Yes," I said, "it will take a half-hour to drive up there." She tucked her arm in mine and we were on our way.

I was real anxious to get there. Not so much as to get it over with, but to see what kind of a performance Billy would be putting on. I was quite relaxed, due to Ireene's lovey-dovey mood. I realized that she would swallow almost any kind of an act today. But Fat Billy the Roofer, I was soon to realize, had completely missed his calling. He would have made one damned fine actor. I truly believe he could have cruised Hollywood with the likes of Gable and Mitchum. To say nothing about Boggart. We pulled in the drive. I went around and helped Ireene out of the Lincoln. The scenes and performance that followed, which I am proudly going to describe to you, were next to none.

The front door to the house was wide open, due to the beautiful, sunny afternoon. As we stepped up on the porch we were greeted with the tune, "Here Comes the Bride," played by piano. (It was actually a tape playing in Fat Billy's tape recorder.) As we entered the front room I felt the relaxed atmosphere of professionals at work. There was now a pulpit sitting in the middle of the room, where my table used to sit. Behind the pulpit stood Billy. Looking very handsome and debonair, in a black suit with large padded shoulders, complete with a black shirt and white collar. A large black Bible with gold gilt edging, sat open on the pulpit in front of him. He was a reverend, all right, if I ever saw one. His expression and manner had actually taken on the personality, of probably, some long dead holy man, whose spirit had come to his aid. Or at least that's the way that it appeared to me. On his left side, stood his wife Sylvia. Looking very attractive in her wedding gown. She was holding a large bouquet of red roses. She was there (as I learned after), to act as witness. As this is compulsory in California. On Billy's right, stood his oldest daughter Gloria. She was eight years of age, and was the flower girl. She was dressed in a floor-length gown, and looked awesome with her bouquet of roses clutched to her chest.

The reverend now spoke in a rich and polished voice. "Good afternoon, my children. Welcome to my home and cathedral."

Now I don't remember the exact wording of the rest of the wedding service. But I have wished a thousand times that I had thought to tape it. The service was quite long. Reverend Bill reading several verses from the scripture. Including, "He leadith me down into green valleys," etc. When he got to the part of knowing me personally, I was afraid that he was taking it a bit too far. As he went on to explain me as an irreplaceable citizen, who was a pillar of strength to the community.

I glanced at Ireene to see how she was taking it. Her expression of complete acceptance and personal serenity told me that all was well in paradise. Billy was now asking for our vows. We said our I do's, and repeat after me's. Then Billy asked for the ring. The ring, I thought in panic, we had completely forgotten about the ring. Sylvia saved the day. She simply slipped off her wedding band and handed it to Billy.

The reverend now slipped it on Ireene's finger. And his golden voice echoed the words, "With this ring you are now wed. I now pronounce you man and wife." And looking me directly in the eye, he said, "You may now kiss the bride."

Ireene was like putty in my arms. *Billy has done too good of a job*, I thought. *It's all real to this gal*. The serene atmosphere was disturbed for a moment. The reverend was asking for the marriage license.

"Oh yes, oh my god, yes," said the now startled Ireene, as she dug it out of her purse and handed it to him.

The reverend now made a big show of scrawling his name and his title across the front of the marriage license with a flourished gesture of hand. Sylvia signed as a witness. The license was inspected by Ireene, and then she carefully replaced it back into her purse. After all, "it was her ticket to freedom." Ireene removed the wedding band from her finger and handed it back to Sylvia. Thanking her profusely for being so thoughtful and kind.

I shook Billy's hand, and said in my best business tone, "Thank you for everything, Reverend, see you on Sunday. Oh, Ireene," I said. "The reverend's fee please."

"Oh my god," she apologized, "I'm forgetting everything today." And then she made a real nice gesture, which I really appreciated. She pulled out two one-hundred-dollar bills. One she said was for the wedding fee, and the other one she presented for what she called a beautifully conducted wedding. And also for the flowers. Billy was grinning from ear to ear now and I knew it was time to get Ireene out of there. As the reverend I knew needed a drink, and was going to have one.

Ireene snuggled up close to me on the way back to Palm Springs. I figured that she was trying to make it seem real just as long as she could. When we reached her apartment building, she said, "Park and come on up for a bit, will you please."

"Sure," I said, "after all it is our wedding day."

"Help yourself to a drink," she called from the bedroom. Five or ten minutes went by. I was listening to Elvis Presley on the stereo. He was singing, "Blue Hawaii."

Ireene called again from the bedroom, "Come in here, Terry, I want to show you something."

I picked up my drink and walked into the bedroom. Ireene was standing beside the bed in her dressing gown.

"It's time to pay up," she said, smiling prettily. She handed me a large brown manila envelope. I opened it up. It contained forty, five-hundred-dollar bills.

"Thanks, Ireene," I said, "that squares us up."

"Not quite," she said, in a near whisper. As I looked at her she dropped the dressing gown to the floor. She now stood in front of me, in black lace panties and matching bra. There was no turning back now. After all, this old farm boy is only human, and damned glad of it.

I awoke at my usual six a.m. Ireene was sleeping with her head on my shoulder. I could tell by her expression that everything was well in paradise. I slipped out of bed without waking her. My first impulse was to get dressed and head for home, and then I thought how ridiculous this would be After all Maggie wouldn't be back until tomorrow afternoon. All my work clothes were here from yesterday. All I had to do was walk across the alley to work at nine. With all of this new knowledge rushing through my brain, I climbed back in bed and woke Ireene. In the most appropriate way that I could think of for a new bride. We decided to get up at eight. Ireene was bustling around the kitchen cooking up my breakfast like a good little wife should.

I got my work togs on, as Ireene called them. I sat down and soaked up all of this attention that I was getting bestowed upon me from those "Unseen Forces."

I walked across the alley to the job, and was greeted by

Chico's smiling face.

"How was she, boss? How was she?" he was asking in a loud whisper, like she might maybe be able to overhear him.

"Who? How was who?" I asked him, playing dumb.

"The blonde big money lady," he said.

"Oh, she was just fine," I said. "Like fine wine."

He now shrieked with glee. "I knew boss," he shrieked. "I knew you fuck her."

"Not so loud, Chico," I cautioned. "She might come down here and whack you one."

"That okay, boss, she can whack all she like," he shrieked again.

"Just get those bricks and mortar up here," I told him with a smile. "We are going to work."

"May not able to work you," he snickered. "Maybe big money blonde take work away from boss today."

"You get those bricks up here or I'll show you what boss can do today," I told him.

We were working in harmony and had gained another two feet on the chimney. When the pleasant female voice came across the alley. "It's lunchtime, sweetie," she was calling gaily.

I could see that little Mex grinning up at me and repeating, "Sweetie, lunchtime, sweetie."

I'll fix him, I thought to myself. "Okay, sweetie," I called back, louder than I had to. "But make enough for three, Chico is coming up too."

The little Mex now looked at me in complete dismay. "I can't go to big money, boss, no not go," he was pleading. "Me poor Mexican, me not feel good up there."

"Shut up and come on or you're fired," I told him.

He looked at me and gulped. I could see that he was now in between the devil and the deep blue sea. Anyway he quietly followed me up the stairs. When we entered the apartment, he stood by the door in awe. I guess it was quite a sight for a man who had never slept on anything except a blanket and a floor.

"Come sit over here, Chico," said Ireene.

Chico sat down at the big walnut table. He looked suspiciously, first at me, and then Ireene.

I started to laugh and whacked him across the back. "Smarten up, Mex," I shouted. This seemed to snap him back to reality and he started to laugh too.

Ireene had fixed us a nice fish and chip lunch, which we washed down with a cold cider over ice. Chico had now regained his composure and just couldn't stop the devil in himself. "Lady Ireene," he said.

"Yes," answered Ireene. "What is it, Chico?"

"Oh, I don't know, lady Ireene. Boss kind of slow today, maybe sick, maybe should go bed early tonight."

I couldn't contain myself, I simply burst into a fit of laughter at this little guy's sense of humor.

Ireene, not knowing the origin of the joke. Put her hand on my forehead, and said, "Are you all right, sweetheart?"

The little Mex was now rocking with laughter. Ireene looked a little confused.

I said, "It's okay, Ireene, just a little private joke."

"Okay," she smiled. Now we all laughed.

"Come on, Mex," I said, "let's get some work done."

It was four-thirty. Chico was cleaning everything up. We had had a good day. At least another six feet of beautiful antique brick chimney was now pointing skyward. Chico was admiring it like he had just built it himself, single-handedly. "Nice, boss," he said, "nice."

I figured that I had better go up to Ireene's and collect my tux. I realized that I had to break this little romance off right now. And was also surprised at myself for thinking that if it wasn't for Maggie coming back tomorrow, staying with Ireene might not be too bad. Ireene buzzed me in.

"What say we go out for dinner?" she offered.

"Got something to tell you, Ireene. Come over here, sit down and listen carefully."

She came over to the table and sat down, looking at me like she knew what I was going to say, but didn't want to hear it.

"The marriage is over now, Ireene," I told her quietly. "You know as well as I do that it was just a business thing right from the beginning. And what we are doing now, is just play-acting."

The silly woman was crying now, which I hated.

"Yes," she confessed, "I know, but I really needed a friend and just wanted to hold on for a while."

"You think you're okay on your own now?" I asked.

"Oh yes," she said, "I'm making arrangements to live in Kelowna, B.C. Stop and see me when you go back to Canada. I'll be in the phone book. Ireene Fraser. I'm sure you can remember the name, sweetie." She just had to add.

I picked up my tux, my patent leather shoes, and left, "the big money blonde," as Chico had named her.

CHAPTER EIGHTEEN

WE SANG IN THE SUNSHINE

Upon reaching Desert Hot Springs, I headed for Fat Billy's cottage. As I pulled in the driveway I could see the fat man was in his usual position. On the front porch in a recliner. A beer in hand. And a twelve-inch grin on his face. "How's the old married man?" he asked through fits of laughter.

"Oh, just fine, Reverend," I answered. We were both laughing now. "Where in hell did you get that pulpit from?" I asked.

"Oh," he said, "it was in the secondhand store where I got the suit. When I saw it I knew it would make all the difference in the world. And so I bought it for thirty dollars."

"Well, I'm here to tell you, Bill," I told him seriously, "you and the girls put on one damned fine show if I ever saw one. Now here's your grand."

I handed him two of the five-hundred-dollar bills from the envelope that Ireene had given me. Billy was grinning from ear to ear, first praise, and now money. Things just couldn't get any better for reverends today. "I still owe you five hundred from Christmas," confessed Billy.

"Not anymore you don't," I said. "You guys went to a lot more trouble, energy and expense for that wedding than what I had expected. So I want you to think of that five hundred as a Christmas present for you and your family. But," I added, "just don't expect it every year."

"I understand," said Billy. "And I appreciate the opportunity to be able to work with a man of your caliber. You know, Ter?" He went on, "There was only one item that we had trouble with. We couldn't find a damned white collar anywhere. And you know what, Ter? Sylvia and I made one out of a white cardboard shoebox, and stapled it together at the back. And all the time I was afraid of the damned thing coming apart. Did it look all right?" he asked.

"It looked real good, Bill. It looked real good to the ones that it mattered to," I told him. "Where's the pulpit?" I asked. "You didn't leave it at my house, did you?"

"No, no, I wouldn't do," laughed Billy. "It's right in my living room with the Bible on top of it. Just waiting for the next marriage. Got any idea when I should schedule the next one for?" he asked. He was now rocking back and forth in the recliner, and howling with laughter at his good fortune.

I picked Maggie up at the bus terminal the following day. We were really glad to see each other. But I could sense a big change in this beautiful lady. She was becoming a little more distant as time went on, and I could see big changes coming up in the near future.

"I promised Guy that I would go up to Big Bear and see him today," I told her. "Do you want to make the trip with me, or are you tired of traveling?"

"I want to stay home today," she stated. "With you, can't you call Guy and tell him that you will make it next weekend. I have got important things to talk to you about," she added.

"Okay, Maggie," I answered her quietly. "I'll call him right now." Which I did.

Guy gave off the idea that he was being a bit neglected, but agreed and said, "Okay, Ter, see you next Saturday."

Maggie now began her tale. She had just enjoyed a long and very interesting two-year holiday. And visiting Los Angeles had made her realize how much she was missing the life that she had left behind. She wanted to go back to her old life and to her old job as a therapist. She wanted to know if I would adopt the city life and move back to Los Angeles with her.

"Well, Maggie," I said, "speaking from the heart, there is no considering to do. Los Angeles is not for me, and I can understand you wanting to return. It's like you just said, we have had one hell of a two years together. But I guess it is just simply time to move on. I'm going to tell you of a song that is in the back of my mind," I told her.

"It is entitled, 'We Sang in the Sunshine.' It was a big hit of the years 1964 and 1965. And sung by a new artist at the time. Her name was Gail Garnet. And the lines that I would now like to refer to went like this: 'Although I'll never love you I'll stay with you one year. And when our year has ended and I have gone away. You will often think about me, and this is what you'll say. We sang in the sunshine, yes we laughed every day. We sang in the sunshine, then I went on my way.'

"This little verse," I explained, "not only describes our situation, but can also act as a guiding direction for our feelings."

The soft-hearted Maggie was now crying softly to herself. "Yes, it describes the way things are for us," she admitted through her tears. "But the one line is wrong. I do love you very much, Terry Fraser. And I am going to have a real hard time leaving. But there is just no point in me tagging along after you any longer. Do you understand?"

"I understand perfectly well, Maggie," I assured her. "Just keep that song in the back of your mind, and whenever you are ready to go I will drive you back to Los Angeles."

She now cheered up a bit, and seemed relieved that this part of the break up was over.

"But you will promise to keep in touch with me, won't you?" she asked. "Aunt Betsey wants you to know that you can keep your motor home on her back property as long as you want to. And I will always wonder what happened to Mr. Morningstar. Now don't you forget about me. Promise me now," she demanded.

I promised her on my mother's grave. Stack of Bibles, and the whole bit. Anything to get her cheered up some. Grief, I don't think becomes anybody. And it definitely didn't wear well on the beautiful Maggie.

I worked hard the next week. The little Mex and I enjoyed every day of it. We had watched as the moving truck loaded up Ireene's belongings and trucked them away. But we never saw her, I guessed that she had probably driven out in the night.

"Where big money blonde go?" Chico asked.

"Oh I don't know, you know how unpredictable women are," I answered. He looked at me, and I could see that he didn't believe me.

We finished the chimney off at Friday noon. I got Fat Billy to come and truck the scaffolding back to the rentals for me. "Chico," I said, "you come with Billy and I. First I have to go to the bank and cash this check, and then I'm taking you boys for lunch."

The Mex sat in the front seat of the Lincoln, as proud as a king. "First time I ride big black car," he stated, through his wide grin. "Put top down, boss, put top down."

I unlatched the canvas top and rolled her back, old Chico was now in heaven. I drove down to Rancho Mirage and stopped at Restaurant Row, where we wined and dined with the finest that money could buy.

The service being to the exquisite. Two hours later I paid the bill and left, the bill spoiled $300 but was worth every cent.

Since I was going to Big Bear City to see Guy on Saturday, Maggie and I decided that she should pack her stuff into the Lincoln, and we would continue on down to Los Angeles, after my visit in Big Bear. We were now on our way. It was midmorning.

"Want to stop and say goodbye to Bill and Sylvia?" I asked.

"No," Maggie answered, "this is hard enough without anymore goodbyes."

"Yes, I agree with you," I said, "I don't like them either."

Big Bear Mountain's east pass was a bit icy, but everything went quite smoothly as the sand trucks had been out earlier that day. We cruised past the Black Betscy, looking more alone and forlorn, under its blanket of snow.

"You know something, Maggie?" I asked. "Every time I pass that old roadhouse I can still hear those boys playing that beautiful Mexican music that they played so well."

"I can too," she said sadly, "and I just know that Ali will get in touch with you soon."

"Sure he will, Maggie," I assured her, and did believe it myself. But I told her, "I think we would have a hard time convincing Guy about that." We both shared a laugh over that one.

Maggie stayed with Auntie, and I headed down to the Crazy Horse to see Guy. "Time you showed up," said old Guy with a big smile. "There was a damned good-looking lady in here to see you about one hour ago. I told her that you would be here sometime today, and she said that she would be back."

"What did she say her name was?" I asked.

"Conchita, that's what she called herself, Conchita, looks like a breed, but damned pretty," said Guy.

“Oh yes, I know who you mean,” I answered.

“She left a phone number for you too, where the hell did I put it?” muttered Guy, as he rummaged around under the bar. “Oh, here it is, yes this is it.” He handed me a piece of paper with Conchita scrawled across it, and a phone number below the name.

“Let’s grab a couple of beers and go into the office,” Guy suggested.”

“Sounds good,” I answered. We sat down at the office desk.

“What the hell do you think we should do about that god damned little double crossin’ Mexican, Ter?” he asked.

“You know what I think, Guy?” I answered levelly. “I don’t see where there is a hell of a lot that we can do about it. With that kind of money, that you figure at 18 million, it would be next to impossible to find him in Mexico, if he’s even there, or any other place for that matter.”

“I was thinking the same things,” said Guy, “but I didn’t want to admit it to myself. I thought about hiring a good detective agency, but I’m afraid that would be throwing a lot of good money after bad.”

“Yes I agree with you on that one, it would only be a waste of money and time. But listen, Guy, I know that you are going to find this hard to believe, but I think Ali will contact us. You haven’t told anybody about the robbery, have you?” I asked.

“No, no, not a soul,” he said.

“And do you know if the law has connected the tunnel in any way to the gold robbery?” I asked.

“Not to my knowledge,” said Guy. “It’s been so long ago now, all those old guys are dead. And the records are probably buried in three feet of paper,” he retorted. “No, Ter,” said Guy earnestly, “it wouldn’t be to my advantage to mention it to anyone. I just said that I would, so we could shake a little gold out of that god damned little replica of a Mex.”

“Yes, I understand,” I told him. “Just keep everything under your hat for now, Guy, I'm more than sure Ali will contact us as soon as he thinks it's safe to do so. I know that he appreciated everything we done for him. Even Maggie thinks so and she is really good with premonitions." I told him that Maggie and I were going our separate ways, and I was that day, driving her down to Los Angeles.

"I'll be god damned," he said, "I'll be god damned, I thought you guys were a lifetime item."

"Gotta use your phone, Guy," I said, and dialed up Conchita's number.

"Oh, my love of my life," she was shouting, "is that you for sure?"

"Yes, yes, it is," I assured her.

"Are you at the Crazy Horse?" she asked.

"Yes, I am," I answered.

"I'm coming right down," she said.

"No not today, Conchita." I explained that I was on my way to Los Angeles today. "I want to meet you here at the Crazy Horse at high noon tomorrow. And you know what?" I went on without giving her a chance to answer, "I'm taking you on a holiday, just you and I."

"Where, where to?" she asked.

"I think Vegas for a start," I said. "Look, Conchita, be here tomorrow, I'm going to have to run now."

"Don't you forget," she was saying excitedly.

"I will be here," I told her, "bye now."

"Oh, I see how it works now," said Guy with a laugh, "one beauty going and another one coming."

"Well," I said, "that's the way it seems to be working this time." And we both laughed.

I collected Maggie and headed down the hill to Los Angeles. We stayed in a second rate motel that night, as Maggie was moving in with a nurse from the clinic, until she found herself an apartment. It was Sunday morning when I dropped her at her friend's and got the luggage unloaded. It wasn't easy leaving this beautiful lady, but we both knew that the time had come. She hung onto me for a real long time, but didn't cry.

"Remember the song I was telling you about, dear," I told her.

"Yes," she said quietly, "we sure did sing in the sunshine, didn't we, Ter?"

"Yes, Maggie," I said, "we sure as hell did."

I turned quickly, got in the Lincoln and left without looking back.

CHAPTER NINETEEN

A MESSAGE FROM ALI

I pulled into the Crazy Horse parking lot, it was twelve-twenty. I was twenty minutes late for my rendezvous with Conchita. I walked on in. The old saloon was doing a roaring business for this early on a Sunday. The gorgeous Conchita was seated at a table halfway up the bar, she was now smiling and waving at me. Guy was her companion at the table. Since learning that she was my friend, he had taken it upon himself to befriend her also. And I knew that deep down inside, he did appreciate a beautiful creature like Conchita.

Conchita was all hugs and kisses. "How do you like my new boyfriend?" she said gaily, pointing towards Guy.

"Well, I think you had the best man in the house," I laughed, "that was until I walked in." We all laughed now. Guy was taking the day off, he had stubbed his big toe on the table leg last night, he told us, and it was just too damned sore to hobble around here all day.

"Well then, comrades," I said with gusto, "let's get pissed."

Conchita liked music, she got quarters from Guy and walked over to play the jukebox. Every healthy male in the place had their eyes on her as she swayed that gorgeous body across the barroom.

"Poetry in motion," said Guy grinning, "you're one lucky son of a bitch with the ladies, Ter," he said.

"That's it exactly, Guy," I said, "let's just hope it don't turn fickle on me."

Conchita was playing Jimmy Reeves. He was giving us "The Sound of Distant Drums." Conchita came back to the table and sat beside me, leaning her cheek against mine.

"Tell me about our holiday, Ter," she said, "I'm so excited that I couldn't sleep all night."

"Can you take some time out from your job?" I asked her.

"That's up to me," she said smugly.

"Okay, sweetie," I told her, "phone them and tell them that you are gone for a month."

"You can use the phone in the office," Guy told her, "come with me."

No sooner had they left than a man in a courier uniform came in. He talked briefly to the barmaid, who I could see had directed him to our table.

"You Terry Fraser?" he asked.

"Yes, I am," I answered.

"I have a parcel for you," he told me. "But the sender gave strict orders that you would have to show picture ID to get it. And in the case where you couldn't conform with this request, I was given strict orders not to deliver."

"Okay, okay," I said, "that's me and I have picture ID." I pulled out my driver's license, which he gave a thorough scrutiny.

"Okay," he said, "I'll be right back."

He came back with a wooden box, approximately sixteen inches by sixteen inches and set it down on the table. "There you are, sir," he said. I thanked him and looked at the box. It was addressed to: "Terry Fraser only," in care of the Crazy

Horse Saloon, 2031 Center Street, Big Bear City, California, U.S.A. That was it, no return address. I picked it up, it only weighed about twenty pounds. Guy and Conchita came back from the office.

"Where in the hell did that come from?" asked Guy with surprise.

Conchita read the address out loud, "To Terry Fraser Only, in care of the Crazy Horse Saloon. Where's it from, sweetie?" she asked.

"I don't have a clue, a courier just brought it in for me," I said, "but I think that we had better go back in the office and find out."

I picked up the box and we all walked into the office. Guy locking the door behind us.

"Got a screwdriver, Guy?" I asked. "This damned thing is nailed shut."

He rummaged around and came up with a small pry bar. I pried the lid off, we were all very curious about what was in this suspicious looking wooden box. I pried the wooden top free of the box. On top of the box's contents was a large envelope, addressed to: Terry Fraser and Guy Simcoe. With instructions to open and read together.

"Looks like I came to the right place today," I said.

"Here, Guy," I said, handing him the envelope, "you do the honors."

Guy tore it open hurriedly and pulled out the letter, he unfolded it and read out loud. "'To my two partners Terry and Guy.' Why that god damned little bastard," he muttered.

"'To my two partners, Terry and Guy,'" he started over again. "'My humblest apologies for leaving quick, but I had to do this. You see I had already found the gold when you two partners came to me with the deal. I had to pretend to like your deal to keep you quiet, Guy. And, Terry, it makes me real sad to have to fool you also, as you were my friend when I needed one, and it make my heart hurt. I laugh at Guy being cold with metal detector, as he was the one to make trouble with his elephant memory, but I don't laugh at you, Terry, only sadness feel. And, Terry, believe it or not, the old army mine detector is much better than what you think, it was with it that I find gold, before you even buy new one.'"

Guy looked at me in disbelief. "Imagine that little son-of-a-bitch," he said, then his attention went back to the letter.

"'I couldn't give you guys half gold, gold not just for me, it is mostly for my fellow man in Mexico. You see I am setting up a new movement that will supply the poor and unfortunate with food each day. For this I need all gold. But I did send something for fooling you, and hope forgiveness. Terry, please get Guy to forgive. Viola sends love to you and Maggie, and I do too, Terry. Share equal what's in box. Your friends till death, Ali and Viola.'"

Guy put the letter down on the desk. He had a real complex look on his face. I would say somewhere between a laugh and a cry. "What's in the box, Ter?" he asked quietly, looking at it like he expected a rattlesnake maybe to spring out.

I tried to pull it out, but it was wrapped in heavy brown paper, and was the same size as the box so I couldn't get my fingers down the sides. I turned the box upside down and shook the contents out onto the desk. A big square package, wrapped tightly with brown paper, plopped out on the desk. I took out my penknife and sliced the paper down the sides. The brown paper fell aside, revealing a nice neat stack of $1000 and $500 American bills.

"Well, I'll be god damned," said Guy, "that conniving little bastard."

"Come over here, Guy," I said, "we will count together."

I counted each thousand and then I passed it to Guy, I marked each thousand on a pad on the desk, as Guy was also doing. Conchita was looking on with big beautiful eyes of disbelief. "Well that's it, partner," I said, "I counted $300,000."

"Right you are," said Guy, "I came up with the same. Hang on," he said, "I'm going out and grab a bottle of brandy, I need a drink, we all need a god damned drink," he added.

He was back in a flash with a bottle of loganberry brandy and three glasses. He slammed the office door, and double locked it this time. He poured out four-ounce sized drinks, and I could see that his hands were shaking. We clinked glasses and took a big gulp. "I'll be god damned," said Guy again, "that conniving little replica bastard, you gotta give him credit, you've gotta give him credit."

We finished our first drink, so I poured us another, only two ounces this time.

"I never saw so much money in all of my life," said Conchita in a half whisper.

"Probably you never will again either," I told her.

"Here," I said, "a souvenir for you." I took a thousand-dollar bill off the top of the stack and poked it into her cleavage. She sat there with her drink in her hand staring down at it. Guy was giving me a questioning look. I looked at him and shrugged.

"Easy come easy go," I said, with a big smile. This seemed to break the spell and we all laughed and relaxed.

Guy sat down in the easy chair next to Conchita, still saying, "Well, I'll be god damned."

Being as I was sitting at the desk I said, "I'm going to split this in two, partner, and you can count your pile when I am finished, okay?" I asked.

"Yes, yes, sure, Ter, you go ahead," he said, as he leaned back and lit a smoke.

"You count with me, Conchita," I said, "that way we double check it."

We counted out $149,000 American dollars. "The rest is yours, Guy," I said.

"Could you lend me a briefcase to lug this out of here in?"

"Yes," he said, getting up and rummaging through the shelves.

"Here you are," he emptied the contents of a large black briefcase out on the floor and handed it to me. Conchita stacked the $149,000 neatly into the briefcase and sat there staring at me.

"What's the matter with you?" I asked her with a smile.

"Nothing," she said, "I just wanted to look at you, is that okay?"

"Sure, sweetie," I told her, "of course it's okay."

Guy opened up his six-foot tall office safe and stacked the $150,000 inside, slammed the door and spun the dial.

"Well, Guy," I said, "you read the letter with me, are you going to be able to forgive Ali for outsmarting us?" Guy looked at me without saying anything, as he poured us another drink from the quart of brandy.

"You know something, Ter?" he said, as he took a sip of his brandy. "I have got to admire that gutsy little bastard. Of course I forgive him, he sent us that money, he didn't have to do that if he didn't want to. Yes, Ter, of course I forgive him, as a matter of fact, let's drink to the little replica."

We clinked our glasses. "To the little replica," I repeated, "may God be with your new project."

"Yes," repeated Guy, "may God be with your new project."

"Just one more thing I have got to ask you for, Guy," I said.

"What's that, Ter?"

"I want to use your phone to call Los Angeles. I think it is only fair that Maggie should hear about this, after all, she did seem to know that Ali would contact us."

"Yes, sure, I insist," answered Guy.

I got Maggie on the other end of the line, and I know that I couldn't have given her a better present that day. I gave her the whole story and read the letter to her, word for word.

"God bless them," she said.

"Okay Maggie," I said, "I thought it important that you knew."

"It sure is," she said. "Now if we can find Mr. Morningstar I will rest easier."

"We will, Maggie," I told her, "don't you worry."

"Goodbye and I miss you," she said.

"Goodbye, Maggie," I said, "I do too."

I put down the phone.

"Who's Maggie?" was Conchita's question.

"Just a lady I used to know, Conchita, just a beautiful lady, something like you," I said with a smile. She smiled back and never asked again.

CHAPTER TWENTY

RENO CARSON CITY AND VEGAS

"Got any summer clothes with you?" I asked Conchita.

"No, but I can soon get some," she said, waving the $1,000 dollar bill that I had given her.

"Well okay," I said, "we are heading for the desert, let's go by the hotel and get your luggage.

"Well, Guy," I said, "it's been quite a day."

"It sure as hell has," he said. Better take that metal detector with you that you bought, it's in the closet there behind you."

"No keep it, Guy," I said, "you never know when you will want to go treasure hunting."

"And probably with a Mexican," he laughed.

"Yes, keep it as a souvenir, I can afford it today," I laughed.

I locked the briefcase in the trunk of the Lincoln and we went and rounded up Conchita's luggage, and were Desert Hot Springs bound. As we passed the Black Betsey in it's eerie silence, I began to brief the fascinating story of its colorful past history to Conchita. So that she could better understand the source of the stack of bank notes that she had so admired on Guy's office desk earlier that day.

By the time that I had completed the story we had finished our descent of Big Bear Mountain, and were in fact, only a few miles from Desert Hot Springs.

"What a story," said Conchita, in genuine amazement. "You know what, Ter?" she said excitedly. "You could sell a movie about that story."

"Yes, Conchita," I said thoughtfully, "perhaps some day I will."

I had also informed Conchita as to Fat Billy's true marital status, and cautioned her in mentioning her friend Linda to Billy, if Sylvia was present. With this all understood, I felt relaxed about pulling into Fat Billy's driveway and stopping to say hi. Conchita was needing to use the bathroom, as we hadn't made a stop since leaving Big Bear.

Our knock was answered with a loud voice from inside. "Come on in, you're out."

As we stepped inside I could see that the pulpit was still taking up its place in the front room. Billy and Conchita said their hellos. Conchita headed in to use the rest room.

"What are doing with that gorgeous Conchita?" Billy asked, with his eyes bugging out of their sockets. "Where's Maggie?"

"Oh, Maggie and I split last week," I told him.

"Well, I'll be damned," he said, with a look of confusion on his face.

"Why didn't Maggie stop and say goodbye," he wanted to know.

"Well, I did mention it," I told him truthfully, "but Maggie just doesn't handle goodbyes well at all."

"Oh, I see," he said, looking a little clearer of mind now.

Conchita was back, and informed me that she was anxious to get home, and in fact, to see her new home. So we bid the fat man, who was now all eyes, a good night.

"What's that pulpit doing in your friend's house?" asked Conchita, "with that big Bible on top of it."

"Oh, I think Billy's learning to be a priest, he's taking one of those correspondence courses," I told her.

She looked at me a bit puzzled. "Can you do that?" she asked in disbelief.

"Oh yes," I assured her, "this is California, they do everything here."

"I guess," she said with a big smile and forgot about it.

Conchita was an early riser and got up at six a.m. with me, but she wasn't a runner, so I done the mountain solo that morning. I was remembering the big diamondback sleeping on my chest, as I always did when passing that spot on the steep hillside. I returned to a beautifully prepared breakfast, prepared by an equally beautiful lady. We took our coffee out onto the porch and I introduced Conchita to her 8 new pets, the roadrunners.

The birds acted a little standoffish this morning. They instinctively realized that Conchita wasn't Maggie, and were a bit wary of her at first, but it didn't take them long until they accepted her presence, and were in fact, taking turns jumping up on her knee and greeting her, in roadrunner language of course. I explained the roadrunner's purpose to Conchita and could see that she immediately held them in a category of high friendship and respect. I also shared the story of old Paul and Sarah next door with her. And all about the great laugh we had with them, and a girlfriend that I had at that time, was the way I explained Maggie to her.

"Did you happen to bring that beautiful red bikini with you?" I asked her.

"Yes I think it's in my suitcase," she said, "why do you ask?"

"Oh," I said gaily, "why don't you go put it on, I'll call over and see if Paul and Sarah are open to a pool party this morning."

"Okay, you devil," she laughed and disappeared inside.

"Hello, is that you Paul?"

"Oh, hello neighbor," he said, "what's up with you this morning?"

"I was just wondering if you were home or not," I went on. "I got someone here that I would like you and Sarah to meet."

"Yes, Terry," he said, "yes sure, come on over, we are out by the pool."

"Okay, Paul, see you in a minute."

Conchita made her appearance in that little red bikini, she was one hell of a sight to behold, all sex and plus. I wouldn't say she was better looking than Maggie. But she was much younger, and being quite a bit taller, she would probably prove more appealing to some individuals. I grabbed a bottle of California white and we headed over.

"The old guy won't maul me, will he?" she asked.

"No," I said, "he would probably like to, but Sarah never goes too far away."

"Well, he better not," she said laughing gaily.

As soon as we rounded the corner of the filter house and stepped out onto the pool deck, I could see my plan was already in motion. Old Paul was transfixed, mouth wide open, leaning forward in his chair, eyes protruding from their sockets.

Conchita, a professional model, now crossed the open deck with "poetry in motion," and a smile as big as Desert Hot Springs on her pretty Navajo face.

"Paul!" I spoke loudly to jar him out of his trance. "This is my friend Conchita." I touched his shoulder, this snapped him out of it.

He was immediately on his feet and had Conchita by the hand, introducing himself as Paul J. Franklin, and kissing Conchita's hand in the process. "Sit right down here, my dear," and he pulled up a chair next to his, his hungry eyes never left her.

Sarah came out and greeted us with, "Good morning to all.

Very pleased to meet you, Conchita. And it's about time you came over, Terry, we haven't seen you since New Year's. And, Paul, what's the matter with you? Can't you see that they have got a bottle of wine? Go get the ice cooler, and get a fresh tray of glasses, these ones have been out here for a month. Come on, Paul, what's the matter with you?"

Old Paul got up and went to do her bidding, and I noticed, with backward looks in the direction of the lovely Conchita. Paul brought out the champagne bottle cooler, put the California white into it and added the ice.

"Oh, the glasses," he muttered, and turned back to the house to get them. Every time that I looked at that damned ice cooler, it was all I could do to keep the laughter back, with the remembrance of old Paul taking his unprepared dive with it, during his introduction to Maggie.

Paul returned with the tray of glasses. I could see that he was walking straighter than usual, with his gut sucked in. *Like a soldier on parade*, I mused to myself, *or better yet, a bull elk in rut*.

"Paul," said Sarah, looking at his foolish show of sex appeal, "is your back bothering you again?"

"No," said old Paul, "my back's not bothering me."

"Well, smarten up," she nagged on, "quit walking that way."

I looked at Conchita, she was also close to exploding with laughter. I turned away, I knew if I looked at her smug grin any longer, I was going to burst out in a fit of laughter that I wouldn't be able to turn off.

Old Paul poured four drinks and put them on the tray. Serving you know who first, with a lingering look and a "Here you are, pretty lady."

Conchita was bad, she answered with, "Thank you, handsome waiter."

I could see that these last two words had bit him right to the quick, he now spun around to serve Sarah and I.

"Thanks, Paul," I said, "you sit down now and enjoy the wine, I will do the honors."

"Okay, Terry," was his ready reply. And as he sat down I noticed he dragged his chair a little closer to Conchita's.

We were now on our fourth drink, and the bottle of California white was gone, as I had been pouring them extra large today. I excused myself, and told them that I would dash home and get another bottle. No one objected. "Bring the sunscreen too, will you, Ter?" asked Conchita.

"No, no," said Paul, almost shouting, "I've got lots of sunscreen here, what kind do you use, pet?" he asked her.

"Got any Coppertone, pet?" she mimicked him, but he never caught it. He was on his feet and rummaging through the bar cupboard for the, now precious, Coppertone.

I was back in a flash with two more bottles of California white, and poured a very generous drink for all, especially Paul's glass. He came back with the Coppertone in hand, and a smile as big as Los Angeles. I handed him his glass, he took a large swig, and said, "And I thank you, sir."

I could see that the old guy had reached the plateau where Sarah and I no longer existed. There was just him, Conchita and the wine, and the beautiful California sunshine that soothed us all.

I walked over to Sarah and told her a foolish little joke, so that I could laugh without being too obvious. I will now share this joke with you and hope that you haven't heard it before.

Now picture this…

A frog hopped down the street and stopped in front of the Bank of America, he hopped through the open door and up to the receptionist's desk. There was a big name sign on her desk telling us her name was, "Patty Black." Patty Black looked at him and said, "What can I do for you, Mr. Frog?"

"I want to borrow $10,000," said Mr. Frog.

"Well, I don't know," said Patty Black, "we have never

made a loan to a frog before. Do you have any collateral, Mr. Frog?"

"Yes," was his firm answer, and he dug in his little back pack and came out with a frog-sized cup and saucer. He handed this to Patty Black and said, "You take this to your bank manager and I'm sure he will lend me the money."

"Okay," said Patty Black, feeling a bit embarrassed at taking this miniature cup and saucer into her manager's office.

"Yes," said her manager, "what is it, Patty?"

"Well," she told, "there is a frog out there and he wants to borrow $10,000. He said if I gave you this that you would grant him his loan. What is this anyway?" she asked her manager.

Now the manager looked at her in disbelief of her ignorance. "What is it?" he exclaimed. "Why it's a nick knack Patty Black give the frog a loan."

Sarah and I were enjoying a real good laugh, when all of a sudden all hell broke loose in paradise. First we heard. "SPLASH."

Then Conchita shrieking, "Don't you ever try that again, you god damned pervert."

Now I was looking at a scene to behold. Old Paul was just coming up for air in the pool where Conchita had obviously pushed him. He wore the expression once again, of a dog coming home to a whipping, among other mixed emotions.

Sarah rushed over to Conchita. "What's the matter, dear?" she asked, now very excited. "What did he do?"

"He insisted on putting sunscreen on my back," Conchita said through her obvious anger, "but he kept on right over my shoulders, and onto my breasts, under my top," she shouted.

Old Paul was now treading water in the deep end of the pool and looking nervously in my direction. He didn't know it, but I was the least of his worries, and his troubles were just about to take a real bad turn. Old Sarah grabbed the long-handled pool skimmer, and struck the old guy over the head with it.

Opening up a gash on his forehead.

"Take that, you foolish old son-of-a-bitch!" she yelled. "Come on, dear," she said to Conchita, and led her into the house.

I could see that old Paul was in a state of semiconsciousness, due to the blow to his head, with the combination of a lot of wine, and the seductive charms of Conchita. I jumped in and pulled the old guy out of the pool. I leaned him back in the recliner, got a towel and mopped the blood off of his forehead and out of his eyes. The cut looked much worse than what it really was, I dabbed at it a bit and it stopped bleeding and began to congeal.

The old guy was now back to full consciousness and was looking at me like he was expecting me to attack at any moment. He started with his I'm sorrys.

"No, Paul," I said, "don't worry about it right now, you're going to have to make some kind of peace with Conchita soon, but not now, give it a bit of time."

"Yes, Ter," he said, close to tears. "I'm out of here." He made an unsteady trot in the direction of his Elcamino. He backed out of the driveway and headed in the direction of downtown Desert Hot Springs, and I figured, to the Alibi.

I called Fat Billy on my cell phone and briefed him on what had just happened. "Billy," I said, "I want you to go over to the Alibi and make sure the old guy is all right, as he didn't look too good when he left here, and you're a lot closer to the Alibi than what I am."

"Okay, Ter, I can do that," said Billy, "I'll head right over, I have to get some beer anyway."

"Okay, thanks, Billy," I said, "give me a call and let me know what is happening with the old guy."

"Will do," answered Bill and hung up.

Realizing that the pool party was now over, I took the still full bottle of California white, and crossed over to my own house. Conchita, I now realized, didn't have quite the peaceful nature that I had gotten so used to with Maggie. *It's the breed in her*, I thought to myself, *I'm going to have to be a little more careful with her than I have been with Maggie*. Ten or fifteen minutes had ticked by when the front door opened and in walked Conchita and old Sarah. Sarah started in to apologize as to the obvious when I put my hand up.

"Whoa, whoa, Sarah," I said, "you don't owe us any apology, Paul's going to have to look after this himself, I already told him that he is going to have to make his peace with Conchita."

"Okay," said Sarah quietly, "where did Paul go? Do you know?" she asked, with a worried expression.

"No, he didn't say," I answered, "but my guess would be that he's at the Alibi."

Sarah left with, "Well, I'll talk to you later."

Conchita had gotten over her anger now, and was back to her usual happy nature. "Did you see his face when she hit him with that skimmer?" she said, now laughing at everything.

"I sure did," I said, we now both shared a laugh. "But you know what, Conchita?" I said, "I'm more to blame for what happened than what old Paul is, after all I knew in advance how you were going to affect his hormones, and I also primed him well with 14 percent California white. All we were attempting to do was get a couple of laughs, but it got a bit out of hand. So if you are going to hold a grudge against anyone, it would be more deserving in my direction than anyone's."

"I'm not going to hold a grudge against you, sweetie, or anyone else. I know we instigated it all, and I'm so happy that you are man enough to admit it," she added, as she put her arms around me and planted a generous kiss on my lips.

"All I want to do," she added, "is to make the old guy think that I'm upset enough that he will stay away from me."

"That's my girl," I told her, "the old guy won't be bothering anyone for quite a long time now, if ever." Now we both laughed openly and honestly.

Billy called back, he said the old guy was ready to come home now, but was too drunk to drive, he said that he would drive him home and then I could drive him back to his house.

"Real good work, Bill," I said, "just come on over when you get up here."

I saw them coming through my front window. Bill got out and went around to help Paul, who made the house by leaning heavily on Fat Billy. *Betcha Sarah's happy now*, I thought to myself. Conchita was napping after drinking the wine, so I went outside and got Billy into the Lincoln and on his way home.

"What did the old guy have to say?" I asked him.

"Oh, he was pretty glum when I first went over to the Alibi," said Bill, "but he cheered up a lot when I told him that you had sent me over. 'I guess he's not too mad at me after all,' was what he said. And then," Bill went on, "when I asked him how firm Conchita's tits were, then he really loosened up. I couldn't buy a drink after that, and that's when he really got himself drunk." Now we both had a good laugh.

Another beautiful sunny day in Desert Hot Springs greeted us the next morning. Conchita and I were having our coffee out on the front porch with the roadrunners.

"Know what, Ter?" she asked.

"What's on your mind, Conchita?"

"Tomorrow is January 20th," she said, "and that is my 25th birthday, and I have been thinking it over about you and I going to Vegas, like you mentioned. But I have never been to Reno, and I really want to see it, will you take me there for my birthday present instead of Vegas?"

"I'll tell you what, Conchita," I said, "going to Vegas was only a figure of speech, if you prefer Reno, then Reno it is, as a matter of fact, it being your 25th birthday and all, I say, let's go and see them both."

"When, sweetie?" she was asking excitedly. "When can we go?"

"I was already thinking that we should be on our way at about 7 a.m. tomorrow morning," I answered.

Conchita was now all excited and all plans. "I have to buy a camera. I have to buy jeans. I have to buy shorts and tops. Take me into Palm Springs so I can shop for all of this stuff," was her next request. This we did, and then hit the sack early that night, as we were planning an early start the next morning.

Seven a.m. the following morning found us packed and on the road. The excited Conchita sat next to me all smiles and eyes. She was a very alert young lady, with genuine interest in everything around her. I found her to be very refreshing and an excellent traveling companion, to say nothing about her abundance of female charms. That had been a gift from the gods, in her favor, and also in mine.

We had taken the freeway to Los Angeles, but bypassed this big city by taking the northbound fork, heading for Bakersfield. The Bakersfield bypass flew by us. The road signs were now suggesting Fresno as the next city. Conchita informed me that Fresno was the farthest that she had ever been north of Los Angeles. Fresno flew by, we were now heading for San Jose. "San Jose City Limits," said the highway sign.

"Want to stop for anything?" I asked. "I'm going to have to stop for gas anyway."

"Oh no, sweetie," was her answer, "I just want to keep going and going, I want to see all of the things that I haven't seen before." She was very taken with all of these new and unfamiliar surroundings. "Will you put the top down, sweetie?" she asked.

I gassed the Lincoln up and rolled the canvas top back and we were once more on our way. The road signs told us that San

Francisco junction was next, then Sacramento.

"We got about four hours to Sacramento," I told her.

"And after that we will be heading east over the Nevada border, and the next city in the state of Nevada, will be, none other but Reno," I informed her.

She was now high on life I could see. She asked, "What time do you figure we will get to Reno?"

"Don't matter a damn," I said.

She looked at me with question in her eyes.

"What I mean by that," I explained, "is that it really doesn't matter as everything in Reno goes 24 hours a day and 7 days a week."

Darkness had encompassed the state of Nevada when we finally rolled into Reno. Conchita had been dozing, but was now awake and glittery eyed with all of the neons flashing every color of the rainbow, in every direction that you looked.

"WOW," she said, "WOW, what a birthday present."

We took up residence at the Golden Nugget, which was everything that a person could want. A casino, a hotel, a cocktail bar, and an entertainment stage. We got settled into our suite. Conchita all excited, got herself all fixed up damned pretty in one of her new outfits, and we went downstairs to enjoy life.

Three days rolled quickly by in Reno, we had by now been all over the city, and saw all of the local highlights. We had watched Rich Little do all of his latest impressions. We had also enjoyed an evening with Wayne Newton.

I could see that Conchita had grown tired of playing the slots, she had played the quarter slots for hours and was surprisingly seven hundred ahead of the game. I'm not lucky at numbers, and know it, and so had kept my gambling strictly to a continuous game of Keno, which began a new game on the wall screen every twenty minutes. I was up sixty or seventy dollars on it also.

"How do you feel about things, Conchita?" I asked her that evening. "Think it's time to move on?"

"Exactly what I was thinking and was going to ask you," she confessed. "Reno's nice, I'm really glad we came, but I would like to see something different now." She was lying back on the bed with the U.S.A. road map in front of her.

"See this place," she said, pointing to Carson City with her make up pencil. "That's the place where the TV series, *Bonanza* was made," she went on, "and when I was a little girl my mum and I used to watch it, and you know what, Ter? I loved the stories, and I was in love with little Joe when I was only seven years old," she told me while laughing at herself. "And it looks like it is on the way to Vegas," she said. "Can we go to that place? My mum and I used to dream about going and seeing that big beautiful ranch house where Ben Cartwright and his family lived. Do you think it's still there?" she asked.

"Yes," I answered her quietly, "I'm betting that it will always be there. We can go first thing in the morning, it is only a couple of hours from Reno," I told her. Her eyes were now big with excitement.

"Wow," she said, "all of my dreams really are coming true."

Early the next morning we had our last breakfast in the Golden Nugget, and lugged our luggage out to the Lincoln. I checked my wrist clock, nine-thirty a.m. *Wow*, I thought, *I'm becoming quiet a penthouse man, like what happened to 6 a.m.?* But then I soothed myself with the thought, *Well everybody deserves a holiday.* Conchita was looking gorgeous in black shorts and scanty red top, with matching slip on sandals.

"Put the top down, sweetie, it's a gorgeous day," she added.

She was indeed all smiles and high on life. I rolled back the canvas top and we were on our way. Reno soon became a small collection of boxes in my rearview. We headed south on highway #395, which after a few miles started its steep climb up to Carson City. Which stood a couple of thousand feet off the desert floor, this stretch of road had been named, "The Highway to the Sky." This climb presented no problem for the Lincoln Ford engineers, as the Lincoln that I was driving at that time was powered by a 460 cubic inch engine. But it certainly did run through my mind never to bring that propane fired motor home of mine up this stretch of highway. We made the summit and motored smoothly into Carson City. Conchita was all eyes as she took in everything about this preserved in time little town. From the narrow board sidewalks, to the old-fashioned bat wing doors of the saloons, it truly was a glimpse into our past, if I ever saw one.

We took all of the local tours on a hay wagon, pulled by a team of beautiful black horses. Which included a tour of the silver mine king's mansion, which had also been preserved as original. After the tour was over we took off on foot to explore the quaint downtown section of Carson City.

We entered an old well-preserved saloon, which was now more of a museum than it was a bar. Near the door where we came in I saw this glass display case, which was below the bar, and also a part of the bar. There was one of the biggest gold nuggets that I have ever set my eyes on, sitting in that display case, it was as big as my fist. Behind the bar stood a small old man in cowboy attire.

I looked at the old man and asked him, matter-of-factly, "Aren't you afraid of somebody stealing that enormous nugget?"

His expression never changed, and so swift and smooth was his move that I missed it entirely. Instantly there was a forty-five, God only knows where it came from, pointing at my midsection. The old man just smiled and said, "NO."

And not to spoil a good scene, I simply said, "I see, and good day, sir."

Conchita was now nibbling on my ear lobe, and asking, "Where is Ben Cartwright's ranch house?"

"We will go find it," I assured her, and we did.

It was just a few miles northwest of Carson City. Although the ranch house was impressive, I was really not as enthused as I had been seeing it on the TV series, with old Ben Cartwright and all of the boys adding to the rugged décor. I could tell by Conchita's expression that she was a bit let down too, as she gazed at the well-furnished, but personal empty rooms.

So I said, "Don't you remember, Conchita? Old Ben used to sit right here," I sat down in the big throne like chair that Mr. Cartwright had dictated life from on many occasions. I pointed to the card table and said, "And that's where Little Joe used to sit and talk to pa. Not on a chair like other people do, but up on that table right there." Then I pointed to my left at the overstuffed armchair, and asked her, "And who was always sitting right there in that big comfortable chair?" Conchita was now getting the complete picture.

"That was Hoss," she said in almost a whisper, and then louder with a big smile, "that was big Hoss's chair."

We had enjoyed the ranch scene, but that only lasts so long, and so we drove back to Carson City. We took a room above the museum where that gold nugget was on display. "You know what, Conchita?" I said reminiscently, "If I was as foolish now as I was in my teens, I would cut a hole down through the floor here, and go down and get that big gold nugget that we saw there today."

"Not a chance," she said, "I don't want to travel all the way to Walla Walla to see you."

"Good point," I told her, "let's hit the sack so we can get up early and head for Vegas in the morning."

"I'm with you," she smiled.

But I knew that going to bed early with this little nympho, didn't necessarily mean that you would feel like jumping out of bed so early in the morning. But I grinned to myself, *That's the path I have chosen, and I'm not bitchin.*

Morning was dictated by a gorgeous Nevada sunrise, which entered our easterly window, and whispered to us with rays of gold. Wake up, lovers, it's time to live, lots of time to sleep when you are dead.

We were now in the Lincoln, the luggage was all packed in the trunk. I was waiting for my lady's usual request.

"Put the top down, lover," she said with her gorgeous smile, "we don't want to miss anything."

I rolled back the canvas top and we headed down the southern slope of Carson City Mountain. We didn't know it right then, but we were about to experience the highlight of our adventures on Carson City Mountain.

When you leave Carson City on the south side, you are on highway #7. I would judge it to be approximately two miles down this highway we came into a half-abandoned village. With a road sign calling it Silver City. I looked around and realized that it had been the center of a good silver lead that had been mined a hundred years or so ago, and then abandoned when the lead had played out. It was now pretty well a ghost town, I thought to myself, and wondered in fact if anyone did live here.

A few more shacks passed by, when all of a sudden I saw, "a diamond in the rough." Up on the hillside from the highway, and on my left, was a low narrow shack. About 12 to 14 feet wide, but long, like approximately 45 feet. The outer walls were very low, I would say 6 feet in height, compared to our modern day building code of 8 foot minimum. But it wasn't the shack that had caught my attention. Alongside of the shack sat "a car buff's dream." It was a 1940 Ford pickup truck. Now anyone who knows anything about these babies, knows that they are priceless when in top original condition. And from the road this one looked good.

"Conchita," I said, "I have just got to pull in there and have a look at that old truck."

We cruised up to the shack. There was no driveway anymore, just sand, we got out to have a look. For you people who don't have a mental image of these old trucks, I want to share a little information with you. In 1940 the distinction between the Ford pickup truck, and the Ford car had not gotten that wide. This truck's cab was the front end of a 1940 Ford car, being sliced down behind the front doors, and equipped with a nicely shaped step side box. And the original car, rear fenders and bumper. It was very unique and came with the flat head V8 Ford engine, giving approximately 75-horsepower, at that time. It had sat there a long time I could tell, as the wheels were two-thirds buried in the sand. The body didn't have a dent on it anywhere. The only visible damage on it at all had been done by the blazing Nevada sunshine. The paint, which was black, was badly faded and blistered on top of the fenders and the roof of the cab. Also the glass, which was all there, had become discolored due to the old style attempt at safety glass, which was two panes of glass sealed together by a coat of clear rubber-like plastic that discolored over the years, from sunlight and high temperatures. From a gray to a pale blue discoloration pattern, it was the worst on the windshield. I rubbed the dust off the left side window and peered in, the upholstery was in excellent shape. The side door was locked, I had wanted to get in and check the mileage on the odometer.

"Conchita," I said, "your eyesight is excellent, so climb up in the box and look through the rear window, see what the mileage meter reads."

"Okay, sweetie," she said, as she hopped her pretty bottom up into the box. She brushed the dust off the glass. "7,000 miles," she told me frankly.

"No, sweetie, it can't be, count your zeros properly, it's got to be 70,000."

"No," she said, with irritation this time, "I can see it good and it's only 7,000."

"Okay, okay," I said, "I believe you, come, sweetie, let's go and see if anybody lives here."

And that's when this extraordinary tale began…

When we were approaching the rickety old front steps, I could see a 4- to 5-foot red racer was draped over the top step, enjoying the shade from the old canopy above. Not wanting any contact with this creature, I stomped firmly on the lower step with my engineer boot several times. He got the idea and slithered down and away on the lower side of the shack.

"And a good day to you too," joked Conchita, in the direction of the vanishing snake, as she raised her eyebrows at me.

We climbed the porch steps that seemed pretty shaky under us. The inner door, I could see was wide open, the only thing between us and the inside was a screen door hanging at a dangerous angle to vertical. I wrapped on the screen doorframe and asked loudly, "Anybody home?"

There was a long pause of silence, and then from the recesses of the house came a strong but distant voice. "Come on in, don't step on my snake."

Hoping that the snake the voice was referring to had been the red racer, I pulled open the old screen door and we stepped in.

"Holy Saint Christopher," exclaimed Conchita. As we watched, a thousand flies of some nationality, arose from all of their at ease positions and rallied into one big cloud which took on many forms, but seemed to hold a territory of about three to four feet, the four feet being to the horizontal law.

"Where are you?" I asked loudly.

"Come on, come on through," said the voice.

I looked at Conchita, she looked at me, we started forward. The black cloud of flies seemed to be acting as our usher, and kept a fairly precise distance of approximately five feet in front of us. We passed through a cluttered kitchen, a leisure room, and now a living room. The air was not good in here, an odor and feeling of decay seemed all around us as we got the first sight of our host. There was a large, and what I took to be an oakwood table, in the center of this also cluttered room. At the table, and directly across from us sat a huge old woman. It was hard to judge her height, as she never got on her feet, but I would judge her at least my height of around five foot eight inches. And the weight was also hard to guess, but I would safely say 300 to 400 pounds. As she spilled over both sides of this, seemingly sturdy chair that she was seated on. The hair was long and white, the eyes were a bright blue, but a bit to the cosmo. Her face was slightly bearded, and her huge breasts rested on the oak table in front of her, covered of course by some type of light blue smock that she was draped in.

"Good morning, ma'am," I offered.

"Well, well, well," was her answer of greeting, spoken in a strong and friendly voice. "Where have you been, my children?"

The black cloud now dispersed to its at ease positions, which now gave us a full view of this strange old woman. Her face had taken on a look of confusion as she stated, "You're not Chester, you don't look like Chester."

"No," I told her quietly, "my name is Terry Fraser, and this lady is Conchita Mountain."

"Oh, I see," she muttered, "did Chester send you?"

"No," I told her, "I don't think I know Chester. Why we stopped," I went on, "is that I saw your old Ford truck outside and would maybe be interested in buying it."

"Oh," she said, and gave us a disappointed look. "That's Chester's truck, you will have to talk with him about that."

"Okay," I said, "who is Chester? And when will he be around?"

"Come sit down here beside me," she said to Conchita with a big grin. "I never had a pretty daughter like you, come be my daughter for a while." Conchita smiled sweetly and took the chair, she seemed to understand and not have any fear of the old woman, who was now patting her on the back and telling her that she could stay with her as long as she wanted to.

She now gave me her full attention and informed me, "Chester is my only son, and I bought him that truck for his 21st birthday present." I quickly calculated her age from 1940 and just had to ask.

"You mean you bought that truck in 1940 when it was brand new?" I asked her in astonishment.

"Oh yes," she informed me, "we went down to Reno and bought it for Chester, he drove us back in it. There was Chester, Dad, and I then. Dad died a long time ago, lungs were bad from the mine tunnels, you know."

"How come Chester didn't drive the truck much?" I asked her.

"Oh, he went down to Reno with a bunch of other guys in a Cadillac one night," she told us with a little tear in the corners of her eyes, "and he hasn't got back yet."

"But when was that, ma'am?" I asked her patiently.

"Oh, that was only the year after," she told me, with a tone like I should have already known. "He went to Reno to celebrate his 22nd birthday and hasn't came back yet, but he will, one of these mornings he will walk in just like you did, I thought that you were him," she said, now weeping openly.

"But ma'am," I said, "that was 46 years ago."

My statement I could see went unheard, this lady had lost all concept to the principal of time. She was now fussing over Conchita, and wanted her to stay for lunch. "Well listen, ma'am," I told her, "I really want to buy the truck, so I will tell you what. I'll go down to Reno and find Chester and try and get him home, and we can make a deal on the truck then." She was all smiles now.

"Yes, yes, yes, Terry Fraser," she said. (I was more than surprised that she had remembered my name.) "Go get that bad boy and bring him back to me, I've got to give him a sound threshing for staying away so long."

I gave Conchita the look (let's vacate), and as we turned to go, our ushers, as if by curtain call, again formed their little black cloud and led us towards the screen door and the great outdoors. The old woman was still calling her goodbyes and hurry backs as we descended those rickety old steps.

"My good God," said Conchita, with a tear in her eye, "some people just don't give up, do they?"

"No, sweetie," I told her, "they sure as hell don't."

We boarded the Lincoln and headed down highway #7 in the direction of Vegas. A few miles down the highway Conchita asked, "What in hell, Ter, what in the hell do you figure happened to Chester?"

"I can't give you a carved in stone answer to that, sweetie," I told her frankly, "but I can tell you what my guess would be."

"Tell me," she said, with sad pleading eyes, "I feel so bad for him and his mom."

"This is my guess," I told her. "Chester was a country bumpkin, kind of not ready for Reno. And in 1941 Reno was a full swing gangster hangout. Now I would say that this bumpkin was possibly a little odd like his mom is, and probably unintentionally pissed one of the local tough guys off. Probably for some silly reason that wouldn't much matter in today's society. And I would guess that he has been buried under the sand, somewhere on the desert plains that surround Reno, for all of these years."

"And I just know that's right," sobbed Conchita. She now cuddled up to me and had a god honest cry. And as much as I disliked women crying, my thoughts were, *Those tears are for you Chester, they have been a long time overdue*. And you know after all of these years, I still wonder what ever happened to that damned truck?

What I'm about to tell you, I'm pretty sure never happened in our world. But it worked real good to cheer Conchita up after her unusual experience. I told her that I just knew that on a real bright and moonlit night, if a guy was in just the right place in the Nevada desert, he would in fact, be able to see that beautiful old black pickup truck cruising the highway in the wee small hours of the clock. With a seemingly 22-year-old country bumpkin at the wheel.

Vegas we chalked up to being a repeat of Reno in a bigger and more luxurious sort of way. The highlight being, we did see old blue eyes, Frank Sinatra.

Conchita was being called back to her modeling career in Los Angeles. I could see that she missed it and had driven her back to her apartment in Los Angeles. Her parting speech was, "You know don't you, Ter, we Navajos mate for life."

"Sure," I said, "I know, sweetie."

"Well I know you won't stay here," she said, "so I will let you go for a while, but it's only temporary now mind."

She spoke very seriously and I could see that she meant everything that she was telling me.

"If you don't come back to me when I call, then I will go to you, and it don't matter where it is," she said with an expression that raised the fine hairs on the back of my neck. This is how we parted. I now pointed the nose of the old Lincoln towards Big Bear and whatever.

CHAPTER TWENTY-ONE

THE RETURN OF DONNIE MORNINGSTAR

It was high noon when I pulled into the Crazy Horse parking lot. The outer door was open as usual. Old blue eyes had the floor, as far as the jukebox went, he was giving us, "The Summer Wind." I walked on in to see Guy's grinning face. "About time the cat came back," he laughed. "I thought that beautiful Navajo had gotten the best of you, and had you down on the reserve for keeps."

"No it didn't end up that way, Guy," I told him with a grin, "but god damned close to it. What's the news around here?" I asked casually.

"Something damned important," he said, "last week was spring break for the school kids, you know."

"Yes," I said.

Guy went on, "Well there was two lads here from Palm Springs, their parents have their weekend away cottage up here, you see. Anyway, these two lads got pissed and ran their dad's Cadillac Coupe DeVille into the lake, just above the dam. A car coming from the other direction saw them leave the highway, broke clean through those heavy guardrails. This other car stopped and watched the water, but never seen them come up. Now these witnesses were 67 and 70 years of age and were not going to dive into that dam, but they cell phoned the authorities. Who came right away, and found out that it was too damned deep to scuba dive. That dam is better than a hundred feet down, Ter," he said. "Anyway, it was daylight before they got the pros on the job. They had old Jake there with his big winch truck, and they got him to pull up the Cadillac kids and all. And needless to say they were drowned as dead as mackerel, both of them. But what I want to tell you the most," he said with excitement on his face. When the divers were down there they saw this other vehicle in there too. And so they hooked old Jake's winch onto it and brought it up. And you know what, Ter? It was a Chevy pickup with old Morningstar still behind the wheel with his seat belt still done up. They figured he must have died from a heart attack, or whatever, before he even hit the water. No god damned wonder we couldn't find him. And do you know what, Ter?" he asked and answered all at the same time. "It's been about a year now and Donnie's god damned body was still as good as ever. And you know what else, his god damned eyes were wide open."

"What did they do with him?" I asked.

"Oh, they took him down to the city morgue and his Apache people came and got him the next day. I guess they buried him out on the reserve somewhere."

"Did anybody ever mention that damned tape?" I asked him.

"No nobody mentioned it, but you could check with the morgue, or better yet, why don't you sneak into the vehicle compound and go over Donnie's pickup, that's where old Jake towed it to."

"Sounds like the best idea, Guy," I told him.

"That's what I'll be doing tonight, that's a real mystery tape and I sure would like to learn what is on it."

The vehicle compound was no problem. I had simply

clipped a hole through the backside of the 12-foot chainlink fence, with a pair of bolt cutters that I had borrowed from Guy. There was no dogs and I soon spotted Morningstar's pickup as the overhead lighting was good. The remnants of a year's water vegetation was still hanging from the undercarriage and the side mirrors of the now rusty Chevy pickup. I popped open the side door, the seat and the floor was empty. I opened the glove box that squeaked and complained from the rust that was fast fusing its hinges. *Pay dirt,* I thought as I looked at the stack of cassette tapes, and right on top of the stack was the mystery tape. I recognized it by the hospital clinic's logo where Maggie was working. I couldn't believe my good fortune and made a fast retreat for the Lincoln.

The next morning I took the tape to an electronic store on the Big Bear strip. I wanted the pros to try it as I was afraid of maybe damaging it further by not knowing how to treat it, after its 12-month soak in Big Bear Lake. I told the guy behind the counter that it had been under water for about a year, and asked him if there was anything that we should do to dry it out properly.

"How long has it been out of the water?" he asked.

"About a week," I told him.

"Well, it's dry now," he stated, "either it works or it doesn't, want me to try it?"

"Yes," I told him, "let's try it."

He popped it in and pushed the play button, and much to my dismay it didn't, only the odd weak squawk here and there.

"Looks like the chemicals in the water have eaten it up," he said, "want to keep it or shall I trash it?" he asked.

"Oh," I answered, "I think I had better keep it for a souvenir." I thanked him, pocketed the tape and left. *It looks like Donnie's mystery tape will always be a mystery*, I said to myself. And I knew that I would always wonder just what in hell had been on that tape that had so upset Morningstar, and was a possible link to his death.

I stopped at the Crazy Horse to let Guy know of our misfortune, and I could see that he was just as disappointed as I was.

"Where's the tape now," he asked unexpectedly.

"Right here in my jacket pocket," I took it out and handed it to him.

"Could I hold onto it, Ter?" he asked, with a dumb expression on his face.

"Why's that Guy?" I asked.

"Well I was thinking that part of old Donnie is kind of like inside of this damned thing. And I would like to hide it away up behind one of the barroom speakers, so that he could still kind of be around here. And who knows, Ter? Maybe a few short years down the road, technology may have figured out a way to make it work again."

"It's yours, Guy." I gave him a big comradely grin and added, "I can't think of a better place for it on the face of the earth."

And to my knowledge it will still be tucked up behind one of those barroom speakers in the old Crazy Horse Saloon.

"You going to start up your contracting business again now?" asked Guy.

"Not just yet," I answered, "I have to go back to Desert Hot Springs for a couple of days. I will have to store my furniture and a few other odds and ends that I have to tidy up. But I will be back soon," I assured him and left with, "adios, partner, later."

CHAPTER TWENTY-TWO

THE MAGIC MAN

I was sitting on my porch in Desert Hot Springs enjoying my coffee with my roadrunner comrades. They missed Conchita and were jumping up on the chair where she always used to sit, and were all chirping out the question, "Where is she? Where is she?"

"Yes, yes, comrades," I told them, "I miss her too, but I am going to be just fine and so are you guys."

I was just thinking that it was a real good time to be getting the hell out of the desert, as I could feel old Mother Nature bringing out the frying pan again, when Fat Billy pulled up all smiles.

"They want you down at the Side Road Saloon," he stated.

"What would that be all about, Billy?" I asked.

"Well, I was in there yesterday and had a few, the guy that owns it, Jack it is, he was telling me that he has to get a sand break wall built around his property. He's really concerned because on a real windy day the sand piles up against the west and the north sides of the saloon. And sometimes he can't even get the outside door open, anyway he asked me who he could get to do it and I told him that I would ask you."

"Jeez, Bill," I answered, "I wouldn't mind doing it, but god damn it's getting awfully close to frying pan time again, and I certainly don't want to get caught in that, not laying blocks anyway."

"Well, let's go see when he wants it done then," said Billy, anxious to get me as a drinking companion.

"Okay, I'll go see him, you go ahead I'll meet you there in twenty minutes," I told him.

It was high noon when I pulled into the yard at the Side Road Saloon. I could see that the man truly did have a sand problem as there were several small dunes forming in the parking area. I went in and met Jack, he told me that if the price was right, he would put the project off for a while, and we could do it in the cooler weather. And so with the fear of the frying pan season out of the way, Billy and I went outside to measure up for this future sand break wall.

As we crossed the yard I noticed an army surplus 4-by-4 jeep pull up to the saloon. A small man hopped out and really looked us over with a quizzical eye, he then turned and walked into the saloon.

"Wonder what's his problem?" asked Billy. "Didn't you see the god damned way that he looked at us, Ter?"

"Yes, I did notice that he was acting a little bit out of the ordinary," I laughed, "but let's not worry about him, let's get Jack's fence measured up and then we can go in and have a beer."

This one word, "beer," seemed to capture the fat boy's attention and he became all business. We went in and sat at the bar while I figured up Jack's estimate.

"Better give us a couple of cold ones, Jack," I asked him.

He set them down and we sipped the first of the day. I didn't realize it, but the "Unseen Forces" were at work again.

When we had come back in I noticed that the little guy, who belonged to the army jeep, was sitting at a table by the window and was devouring a plate of eggs and toast. He now came towards us, coffee cup in hand. He perched himself up on the stool beside me, and as a way of greeting, he asked me, "What are you doing in here?"

A thought of "What the hells it to you?" was hovering in the back of my mind, but I could see that it would be to no one's advantage to let it out. I turned and looked at this inquisitive little guy. He was around 5 feet in height, and a very lean approximate 100 pounds. Most of his hair was gone, he was an unattractive person, that was until you looked into those eyes of his. Those eyes were a deep blue in color, and told me immediately of high intelligence, mystery, and danger, mixed with a few other things that I was unable to put an immediate finger on.

"What am I doing in here?" I repeated his question, and with a smile told him that being a brick and block layer, I was here to give Jack an estimate on his sand break wall to be, that would completely enclose his property.

And now much to our surprise and amusement, the little guy flatly stated, "You don't have to do that kind of work anymore."

Now Billy and I were both laughing.

"And why is that?" I asked him.

"Because you're a dowser," he stated, "you're a dowser like I am, you see a good professional dowser can spot another one almost immediately through our shared energy plane of vibrations," he explained in a very intelligent-like manner. "I knew about you as soon as I got out of my jeep and saw you outside," he stated. Billy, I noticed, was now all ears and eyes, but he kept quiet.

"Well," I told him, "that's all fine and dandy, but you will have to explain to me what a dowser is."

"Well," he said, now in his professional tone. "Let's start from the beginning, you must have experienced somewhere along your lifetime, of men finding water wells with a forked stick," he asked.

"Yes," I answered, "you are, I think, referring to a water witch."

"Yes," he answered, "that would be a typical slang title for the procedure. The actual professional title is 'A Water Dowser,' not a water witch," and he went on. "Where in your past did you connect with this so-called water witch?"

"Oh," I told him, "that was back in Ontario, Canada, when I was a kid, I used to do this myself. I used to take a forked stick and find water wells for the farmers back in the country where I grew up."

"I knew it, I knew it, didn't I tell you that you were a dowser." He was grinning from ear to ear now, showing us a good set of store bought teeth. "And how," he asked, "did you find out that you could do this?"

"Oh," I said, "that was as accidental as running into you today. You see, when I was around 16 years old, I had always wanted a Bulova wristwatch, which was top of the line at that time, as you probably already know."

"Yes," he nodded, "go on."

"Well, I saved for a long time to buy this watch as I was only a sawmill worker at that time and wages were only seven dollars per day. Anyway the good day finally came and I went into the nearest little town, which was called Gravenhurst, and I bought my Bulova watch. And after showing it off for a day or two, I noticed that my so treasured possession was either losing time, or stopping completely. Now very crestfallen, I took it back to the jewelers where I had bought it. And told the man what was happening with it. 'Leave it,' he said, 'and I'll get Albert my watchmaker to check it out.'

"I went back and picked it up the next weekend. 'Can't find

a thing wrong with it,' said the man, 'it all checked out real good, just take it, Terry and try it again,' he said.

"This I did, but it was no better. So back I goes the following weekend, feeling real bad about my watch.

"'It's no better,' I told the jeweler.

"'Okay, Terry,' he said, 'I think I know what the problem is, come on with me,' he said.

"So we took a short drive in the old guy's new Buick, out to a little farm that he had on the edge of town. He cut a Y stick from one of the willow trees that grew alongside the fence. He then showed me the proper way to grasp one of the forks in each hand. He pointed me towards his well and said, 'Hold the stick the way that you are doing and walk slowly forward.'

"This I done, and when I crossed over the water vein that fed his well, all hell broke loose. And in spite of my superior strength of youth, that stick was twisting down in the precise direction of that water vein. It was so powerful in fact that it twisted the willow bark off the two forked ends that were in my grasp.

"'What the Hell!!!' I exclaimed in amazement.

"The old jeweler was now caught up in a fit of laughter due to my expression of utter surprise. He took the stick then and crossed the same spot to show me that it had no effect with him. The stick never moved.

"And that's where I first learned the term," I told the little guy.

"That was when the jeweler then told me, 'You're a Water Witcher, Terry, and there is no wristwatch made that will work on you. But don't worry,' he had also said, 'I will give you your money back, and not only that, I will also get you some water witching jobs.'

"And he kept his word on both counts.

"So there you are Mr. Dowser," I told him.

"Not Mr. Dowser," he said with an air of insult. "Hank it is,

Hank Smythe." (I didn't know it then, but I was soon to learn that Hank Smythe was one of the most highly respected dowser in the U.S.A.)

"And I'm Terry Fraser, and this is my friend Bill Mcphee."

We all shook hands and I ordered another round of beer, which Hank refused and settled for another cup of coffee, and telling us that he never did drink any alcoholic beverages.

"What's your story, Hank?" I asked the little guy. "And why do you think that being a dowser, as you term it, could possibly give me a reason to give up my present occupation."

"Well Terry," he explained, his manner was much more relaxed and friendly now, "my term 'dowsing,' could very well paint a very colorful future for you. Look," he said, "we professional dowsers have taken the power of dowsing far beyond the simple task of finding a water vein for man's use. This dowsing technique is being used through out the U.S.A. and many other countries, to allow man to find metal and mineral veins, lost mines, and best of all," he finished with a big smile, "buried treasure. And do you know what else we are doing now, Terry? We are also doing map dowsing."

"And what does the term, map dowsing tell us, Hank?" I asked.

I glanced at Billy and could see that he was completely captivated by this strange conversation. He knowing even less about the subject than I did, I guess it seemed pretty mysterious to him, all right.

"All right, map dowsing," stated Hank with an air of the mystic, "simply means that I can take a map of Arizona, or any other state, and I can mark on that map where a certain object is buried, while sitting right here in California," he finished with a smug grin.

Billy was now bug-eyed and was muttering, "No, no, impossible."

"Oh no, it's not impossible at all," said Hank in a very

confident tone. We now had Jack's attention too, and he hung on the bar beside us, catching every word.

"I'll tell you what I'm going to do, Terry," said Hank, now in an authoritative tone that did not go well with his stature. "I'm going to give you your first lesson in real dowsing. And you," he was addressing Billy, "you watch closely and stop being a pessimist."

Billy blinked and gulped, but he didn't say anything. I could see that this strange little man some how had him tongue-tied, and a little bit baffled. Hank went into his vest pocket and pulled out an eight-inch length of fine gold chain, with a ruby-like red stone dangling from the one end of it.

"This is called a pendulum," he stated, "and is going to tell me exactly how much money you have in your pockets, Terry," he told us.

"Okay with me," I told him.

Hank picked up the chain, letting the end with the ruby stone dangle down 5 or 6 inches from his thumb and forefinger. The pendulum began to swing from side to side, and then changed directions and seemed to swing the other way. Hank put the pendulum down on the bar, he looked at me and said flatly, "$37."

Taken by surprise along with everyone else, I stood up and turned out my pockets on the bar. $37 it was, a twenty, a ten, a five, and eight quarters.

"Well, I'll be god damned," blustered Billy in disbelief, "how the hell did you do that?" he asked.

"Be patient," answered Hank, "we are not finished yet, now, Terry," he said, "I want you to go in the rest room and put part of your money in your left hand pocket and the rest in your right. Come back out here and I'll tell you how much is in each pocket."

"Okay," I said, and headed for the john, leaving everyone behind me speechless. You could have heard a pin drop in that old barroom when I came back out and sat back down at the bar again. Hank didn't say a word, he simply picked up the pendulum again and seemingly put it through its paces. He set it back down on the bar again. He turned to me and said loudly and firmly, "$10 on the right side, $26 on the left."

Now I stood up and turned out my right side pocket, $10 it was. Now I turned out the right side, $26 it was.

"But, but," stammered Billy, "where in hell did the other dollar go, there was $37 last time."

Hank looked at Billy and said, "Oh, Terry will tell you where that is."

"Yes, I can," I confessed, "I thought I could fool him, I left four quarters under the soap container in the can, you go get 'em, Billy."

Billy camc back with the four quarters and dropped them on the bar, muttering, "Well god damn me, well I'll be god damned if he didn't do it."

I stood up and began to applaud. "Come on, fellows," I said, "let's have a good hand for our new buddy Hank."

Everybody now broke out in cheers and applause. Old Hank, I could see, was literally basking in this newfound attention. Old Billy got up and gave him a comradely smack on the back that damned near knocked the little guy off his perch.

"Easy, Billy," I laughed, "we don't want to lose this guy."

Old Hank now had my respect and attention, and everybody else's that was in the Side Road Saloon that day. The little guy turned to me and spoke in his authoritative tone again.

"And another thing, Terry, you mentioned that your introduction to water witching, as you were then terming it, was as accidental as meeting me here today. Well, I want you to believe this, that meeting me here today was far from accidental. You see I was over in Palm Springs visiting a friend. I drove down from Phoenix yesterday, and when I left my friend's his morning, instead of taking the highway west to

Arizona, I came this way for no apparent reason. But I was in fact, being guided by 'The Unseen Forces,' to seek you out," he stated firmly.

"Okay, Hank," I said evenly, "I do believe what you have just told me, as I too have had past experiences with The Unseen Forces."

"Yes," he said quietly, "I thought that you would have, and now that I have found you," he went on, "I must talk to you in private as I have a story to tell you."

"Okay, Hank," I answered, "you follow my Lincoln, we will go to my house." I could see by Billy's expression that he had just been cut to the quick by those five words from Hank (talk to you in private), but I was very curious to hear what the little guy had to say. So I said, "Catch up with you later, Billy."

Billy answered with a hangdog expression on his face. "Later, Ter."

CHAPTER TWENTY-THREE

THE SILVER DOLLAR ROBBERY

And this is the strange and interesting story that Mr. Hank Smythe related to me on that bright skied and sunny day at Desert Hot Springs California.

It was year 1896 in Arizona. Our story begins alongside Wilcox Lake, which is today, "a dry lake," and is situated as the railroad track runs, a few miles west of Tucson. On this eventful day in 1896 there was a westbound freight passing by Wilcox Lake. This particular train had on board a shipment of freshly minted "Double Eagles," which are $20 U.S.A. gold coins. There were these two stumblebum desperados, who had somehow gained the knowledge of this attractive shipment. And also the knowledge of when it would be passing this location.

These two boys, as the story goes, were not overly bright, but what they did lack in brainpower, they seemingly made up for in guts. Upon knowing the precise time that this, "little bonanza," would be passing Wilcox Lake, they had removed a few sections of rail. And as the unsuspecting train rounded the bend by the lake, they found themselves derailed. And in fact mired down in the sand of the surrounding desert. Our two bozos now overpowered and tied up the train crew.

Before I go any further I want to explain to you that this robbery was well publicized at the time, and entitled, "The Silver Dollar Robbery." As I have explained, it was gold coins that were actually stolen. But the robbery nevertheless was called the Silver Dollar Robbery, and reason being you are just about to find out.

After securely tying up the crew, our two boys headed for the treasury car. Once inside they were preparing to blow the door to the walk in vault. Not being able to purchase anything as sophisticated as nitroglycerine back in those days, they were in fact preparing their charge from black gunpowder. And it being common knowledge, that dynamite, or black gunpowder, must be tamped so as to direct the strength of the charge to where you want the force to work for you. In other words, to blow force into the vault lock, you would have to pile something heavy against the outside of the charge, so as to direct it into the door. Without this tamping, as it is termed, it would blow most of its force harmlessly away from the door.

Anyway our boys understood all of this, and looking around for tamping material, their eyes came in contact with a stack of canvas bags that were filled with silver dollars. There had been no room for them in the vault, and so they had been stacked on the floor of the treasury car. Our boys now grasped opportunity and stacked these bags up against the vault door and their black gunpowder charge. Not being very professional safe crackers, these lads had put double the amount of black gunpowder into the charge than what normally would be used. WHAM!! BANG!!

When this charge ignited and blew, it not only demolished the vault door. But also blew the treasury car apart, sending a hailstorm of silver dollars out and across the desert, which the natives of the area would pick out of the sand, after a windstorm, for many years after. They were also digging them out of the telegraph poles that were near the site where they had become embedded. This is where came the title "The Silver Dollar Robbery."

After the dust settled, our two heroes cast aside the ruble of what was once a treasury car. They retrieved the canvas bags filled with the "Double Eagles." These coins had the face value of $62,000 U.S.A., a lot of money for two stumblebums in 1896. They secured the gold to their horses and made a fast retreat for the Cochise Mountains, via Apache pass. Now the natives of the surrounding area had came to investigate the source of that far heard explosion. And now had formed a vigilante posse, and with the help of professional trackers, were now hot on the trail of our two desperados.

By now our boys were riding very tired horses, as they had gained considerable altitude on Cochise Mountain. They stopped on a flat plateau to rest, and it is thought that this is the place where they buried the gold coins. As they could hear the fast approaching posse. The posse on sighting the two desperados from a distance stopped and ordered their best marksmen, with long rifles, to fire to kill on the two figures ahead. One of the boys was brought down, but the other one, probably having a better horse, got away. When this unfortunate bandit, who had been shot dead, through the back, was identified by the train crew as being one of the robbers. The second one, who had gotten away was also identified, and named to the authorities by the train's fireman, who had apparently known him from years before.

Now as the story was related to me, this second desperado was shot to death in California, less than a year after this episode in Arizona, while trying to rob another train down there. And so it has always been thought that most of the gold coins, if not all of them, were still buried up on Cochise Mountain. The desperado, who had been shot up on the mountain that day, had no gold on his person, or in his saddlebags.

"Now," said Hank, looking at me with those bright mystic eyes of his, "your job will be to help me find that pile of gold coins. If you have any interest in doing so, and I do think that you have the interest. As I have this ever occurring feeling when I look at you." He went on now more serious. "It's a feeling that you were somehow attached to this event, possibly a reincarnation of one of those desperados, and that is why I think, that I was guided to you by the 'Unseen Forces' in the first place. Make sense to you?" he asked abruptly.

"Yes, Hank," I said, "there are a lot of things about life that we don't understand, that yes, I think that you are making perfect sense."

"Okay then," said the little guy, looking real pleased with everything.

"First thing I'm going to do is teach you how to map dowse."

Which he did, and which turned out to be a simple enough procedure, if you possess the talent to do so. We both dowsed the map of Cochise Mountain, so as to establish a general area of where those god coins were buried. And although our dowsing locations didn't match exactly, they were nevertheless, in the same general location on Cochise Mountain.

"Okay," said old Hank, now all smiles, "the next thing for us to do is get ourselves to hell up there," he said, as he jabbed the dowsed area of Cochise Mountain with his index finger.

"When can you go?" he asked.

"Hell I can go tomorrow," I said.

And that is how our treasure hunt for the proceeds of the "Silver Dollar Robbery," began.

"What do I need for equipment, Hank?" I asked.

"Nothing," was his reply, "I got everything in the back of the jeep. Got a one-man tent for each of us. Can you eat like I can?"

"How is like you can?" I asked.

"I eat directly from the can," he answered, "beans mostly, sardines and oysters, this way all you need is a can opener and a spoon," he added.

"Yes, that will do for me too," I answered. And I added, "I never did enjoy camping out that well, as to prepare a full course meal out in the wild."

"My thoughts exactly," agreed Hank, as a kind of confirmation.

"Well you might as well bed down here for the night," I told him. "Then we can take off bright and early in the morning for Cochise Mountain."

"Agreed," nodded Hank. He seemed to be a very happy little man.

We talked on about our travels until 11 p.m. before we retired for the night. Hank, I had learned, had actually led expeditions into the "Mighty Superstition Mountains," in search of the fabled Lost Dutchman Mine. Which he told me, he is fully convinced that it no longer exists, other than in legend. He figures it to be a played out lead, like hundreds of others.

Six a.m. found us locking up my house and climbing into the jeep. Old Hank pointed her east, saying that we would stop in Phoenix for the night, and then get another early start tomorrow.

"I think the best way to do this, Terry," he said, "I got some aerial photos of the area that we want to go into, I think that we might as well both dowse them. And then I'll get my man with the chopper to set us down on that plateau where they figure the boys buried the coins. What do you think?"

"I think that the chopper sounds great," I told him, "not much sense in packing in unless you really have to."

"That's what I figured," agreed Hank, "by the time you get the horses ready, you need two packhorses to pack enough grain for them.

"Okay," he smiled, "it's confirmed then, that's how we will do it."

Old Hank's house in Phoenix was much larger, and a little more deluxe than I would have imagined. I could see a lot of wealth lying around in the form of richly carved furniture and statues from all around the world. His TV room was a miniature theatre, complete with a five-foot screen. He also kept a well-stocked bar and told me to help myself to anything that I wanted, as he just never did drink. So I took advantage of his generous offer and rummaged around until I discovered a nice cold bottle of California white, which was the answer to this old adventurer's prayer after that long and hot ride in Hanks bumpy old 4-by-4.

Daybreak the next morning found us hovering over a section of the Cochise Mountain. Hank and the helicopter pilot, Dave, had decided that this was the spot that we had dowsed on the aerial photos. Dave couldn't set the chopper down due to the pressure from the cold air, and the still warm sand from yesterday had built up. So we ended up being cable dropped a hundred feet or so. I went first with the supplies.

"Watch out for the sidewinders when you hit the ground," Hank warned.

We were now both on the sandy plateau of Cochise Mountain, and Dave's chopper was just a hum in the distance.

"Well, where is it?" joked old Hank.

"Good question," I answered, "what's your usual procedure?" I asked him.

"Well," he said, "your guess is just about as god as mine, it always seems to work out different every time, but this time," he said, "I'm going to start to look with what you used to call a water witcher's stick."

He broke off a forked stick from the mesquite bush next to us, and he said to me, "All you have to do is mentally concentrate on those gold coins, make your stick understand that you are not looking for water, you are looking for gold coins. And if you concentrate hard enough it will get the idea.

"But it's never easy," Hank added, "that's one of the reasons that I have you here with me."

He now asked the stick out loud, from where he was standing, in which direction were the gold coins buried. He began to turn his body clockwise with the stick grasped in front of him. He made about a half turn when the stick went down.

"That's the direction," he said.

He lined himself up with a rock that was a quarter-mile away, and then started slowly walking in that direction with the fork stick grasped in front of him. At about 150 feet from where he had started, down went the witching stick.

"Better dig out that metal detector, Terry, we will check this spot out."

I dug out the detector and took it over to the spot where Hank was standing. I set the ground mineral rejection setting to its proper position and passed it over the spot where the stick had led us, nothing, no beep of gold coins was heard. I looked at Hank and could see that he was unruffled.

"It takes time," he told me, "you never get it right away, it's almost like the Unseen Forces, have to somehow expect you first. Just stay confident," he told me.

I broke off a stick and went to work as Hank was doing. It was now high noon.

"Let's get some beans and go over in the shade of those juniper trees," suggested Hank, "that old gold has been here now for just about a hundred years, another hour or two isn't going to make a hell of a lot of difference."

"Good strategy, Hank," I told him. We found a seat on a

smooth rock under the shade of the juniper trees. We had a couple of cans of beans with the pull away tops, didn't even need a can opener, just a spoon.

"Something that I have got to tell you," said Hank, now looking kind of mysterious, "listen to your feelings, your heart, your premonitions, that is usually the key to the treasure," he said. "And especially you, Terry, watch for a vision and strong premonitions, I think that you have been here before, a long time ago. And I really think that the key is with you, as soon as you are able to find it."

It was getting dusk in the mountains. We pitched our one-man tent on a level stretch of ground. I gathered up a bunch of tree limbs, and dead trees. I hauled them over to the campsite so that we could rustle up a campfire. We got the coffeepot out and had a good steaming cup of coffee.

"There's a shotgun in the big packsack," said Hank, "you go ahead and take it into your tent if you want to," he suggested.

"Oh no," I told him, "I have no fear of the animal kingdom, you keep it."

"Okay," Hank said, "I'm turning in now."

"Sleep well," I told him.

I was getting some unusual and strange feelings inside of me, feelings that I had never experienced before. I got up and strolled over to the rocks where we had eaten our lunch. I sat down on a rock and leaned my back against a tree trunk. I closed my eyes for a moment. A face went past my vision field, a face that I didn't recognize, but a face that was somehow familiar. This face materialized several times, some were of this face in laughter, some in agony and anger. I felt spooky all of a sudden and opened my eyes.

Better hit the sack, I told myself, *if I sleep here the sidewinders will get me for sure*. I climbed into my tent and zipped it up to keep the snakes and bugs out, climbed into my sleeping bag and slept the sleep of the dead. Last thing I remembered was the wolves howling miles away.

Sometime during the night I had this dream, I don't remember what it was all about, but I do remember that same face that I had the vision of earlier that evening, when I had been leaning against the juniper tree. But this time it was different, this time I envisioned not only the face, but the entire man. He was a rugged looking character of dark eyes and dark hair. He was in a kneeling position on the ground, and was digging with a small pack shovel alongside a rock. This all flashed back to me when I was waking.

I could hear old Hank clattering the metal coffeepot, and could smell the beautiful aroma of wood smoke. I climbed out of my sleeping bag and went out to join Hank.

"Coffee's ready," grinned the old guy, "and how did you sleep?" he asked.

"Oh, a very good sleep," I told him, "but I had all of these fleeting visions," and I related to him what I had seen through my subconscious vision field.

"Hmmm," said Hank, "that sounds real interesting. Want to know what I think, Terry?"

"Sure I do," I answered.

"Well, I think that face and that man, that I know you did envision, was one of the boys who robbed the train. And the fact that he was digging beside a rock on his knees, I would bet on it that you have just had a vision of the real burial of those double eagles. So we now know that we should be searching alongside a rock in this vicinity. And you know what else I think, Terry?" He now got real serious and made me feel a bit uneasy.

"Go ahead," I said, "tell me what's on your mind."

"Well," he said, "I don't want you to take any offence of this, but I think you are the reincarnation of either that man that you saw last night, or the other guy who was with him on the robbery."

I looked at him, and somehow knew that he was right. There was now a long pause of silence. Finally I said, "Well okay, I should be able to find this damned cache if I was one of the ones that buried it here in the first place, damned rights. Yahoo. Yahoo," I yelled and danced around the campfire.

Old Hank caught the spirit and started to yell and dance with me.

Everything seemed to go smoother after that. It was kind of like the spell had been broken, or better yet, like we had just been accepted to the mountain.

We spent most of the next day taking turns with the metal detector, alongside the numerous stones that stuck up above the sand.

"What did that stone look like exactly?" Hank asked me at lunchtime.

We were sitting on our rocks under the shade of the juniper trees.

"It looked like most of those rocks out there," I waved my hand in the direction of the plateau, "it was smooth, about three feet long and about two feet high."

"Yes," said Hank, "like most of them out there."

He gazed out across the plateau.

"And you know what else, Ter? That damned whispering shifting sand is forever changing things. Burying some rocks, uncovering other ones, a never ending cycle," he muttered, and looked real sad as he spoke.

It was high noon of our fifth day on the plateau. Hank, I noticed, had withdrawn from me, and had surprisingly turned sullen. So I was spending most of the day just wandering the plateau. Something was gnawing at me, I had those funny feelings inside of me again. But no other visions had appeared since the first night. It was like the spirit world had ushered us up here and then had turned and left.

That afternoon Hank went to the far end of the plateau with the metal detector. It was more like he was waiting for something, than looking for something. I tried to understand his mood, and his personal withdrawal from my company, but didn't worry too much about it.

That evening we got the fire going and the coffee on, I took a can of beans and went and sat in my favorite spot under the juniper tree, as Hank wasn't talking anyway. I sat down, leaned my back up against the juniper tree, and sat munching my beans in tomato sauce… AND THAT'S WHEN IT HAPPENED!!! All of a sudden that gnawing feeling was gone and I knew exactly what it had been trying to tell me. YOU HAVE BEEN SITTING ON IT ALL OF THIS TIME, YOU FOOL!!! I sprang up yelling, "Hank, Hank, bring that metal detector, those damned coins are right here."

Old Hank seemed to know immediately that I knew, and he was moving like a twenty-year-old. He passed the detector alongside the rock that I was sitting on. BEEP, BEEP, BEEP, it was howling to us like a banshee, Old Hank shut it off and set it aside.

"I knew it," he said, "I knew that you could do it, and I owe you an apology. I didn't want to shut you out and pout to myself," he grinned. "But I knew that as long as I was taking your attention, you wouldn't be able to do it. It was just an act," he confessed. Grinning as wide as Cochise Mountain.

The old boy trotted over to the packsacks and came back with the camp shovel. "Now," he said, "let us take a good look at this precious little cache."

Hank was on his knees scraping away at the topsoil. Five inches down, he hit a large root from the juniper tree, it was 6 to 8 inches in diameter, and was right on top of our treasure, almost as if it had grown there to protect what was below.

Old Hank snorted and said, "That damned tree wasn't even

here when those boys buried that gold, what a change time makes."

"Want the axe?" I asked.

"Going to have to have it," he answered.

I went over and retrieved the axe from the woodpile. I got out the flat bastard file and honed it to a fine edge.

"There you go, partner," I said, and handed him the axe.

A few professional strokes of that razor sharp axe and a two-foot section of that root was gone. Hank had a hole approximately two feet in diameter and about a foot deep in the firmly packed sand. Another four inches and we hit it!!! There were four large leather saddlebags on top, the leather bags had held their form due to the sand that was packed around them. But they disintegrated on contact, all of the life was gone from the leather by too many years without oxygen. As the scrapes of old leather fell away into tiny pieces, those beautiful gold coins were exposed to the daylight, as bright and shiny as the day they had been minted.

"Well, I'll be a god damned sidewinder myself!!" shouted Hank. "Did you ever see anything so beautiful? And a hundred years, Ter, they have been sitting there over a hundred god damned years, can you imagine? Please don't touch anything for a minute, Ter, I've got to get the camera and get a picture of this before we go any further."

"Yes," I agreed, "let's do that for sure."

Old Hank took photos from every angle. Got some of me kneeling beside the hole, I took some of him in the same position. I was getting those funny feelings again, I had this overpowering feeling of the presence of others. I looked at Hank and could see that he was feeling uncomfortable too.

"You feel what I feel?" I asked him, a little bit alarmed now.

"Yes," he said in almost a whisper, "it's them. It's the spirits of them two." We looked at each other in silence. Suddenly a strong wind started blowing down the plateau. It whistled and moaned through the trees around us, and then was gone as suddenly as it had came, taking the eerie feeling with it.

Hank looked at me and spoke clearly and loud this time. All he said was, "They are gone."

We got our spare duffel bags out and started the process of double counting the coins and putting them into the duffel bags. The original canvas bags that had once held these coins were now more elusive than what the leather saddlebags had been. They seemed to turn back to earth and dust under our very touch. Beneath the four saddlebags were two burlap potato sacks, which we could see had been tied together, so as to be thrown over the back of a saddle.

"So that's how they got all that gold on two horses," chuckled old Hank, "I was wondering about that."

The burlap fell away into fragments too.

"From dust to dust," I quoted out loud.

Darkness seemed to encompass Cochise Mountain very quickly that night, we were only halfway through our coin counting when we realized that we would have to get our gas lantern out. We finally finished up. I checked my wrist clock, 12 midnight, right on the button.

"What do you make of that?" I asked Hank.

"Seems to fit in here just right," was his answer.

"There should have been three hundred and ten thousand coins there to make up the $62,000," said old Hank. "So it looks like the guy who got away from the posse had $2,000 with him."

"Well, I'm certainly glad that he got something out of it," I said.

"Yeah, so am I," said Hank. "But I thought for a moment that he was back for more, before that wind came whipping down the plateau."

"Yes, I had the same feeling exactly," I admitted.

We had three hundred and eight thousand double eagles

packed into six packsacks. Hank got Dave on the telephone and told him to be there at the crack of dawn, as we were ready to come out.

"Terry," said Hank, now in his authoritative tone, "let's you and I figure out what we are going to do with all of this coinage," he said with a grin.

"What are our choices, partner?" I asked him.

"Well, the way that our politicians would like to see us do it, would be to take it into Phoenix to the Bank of America. There they would give us a big handshake, and possibly a thousand or two reward, and it would then revert back to the crown. Now the only way that we could come out of that like winners would be to sell the movie rights to MGM as it was a well-publicized robbery at that time. Now that could be worth a hundred thousand, or…" He now looked at me with those eyes of his a sparkle and went on.

"Or we can take 'em down to Phoenix and lock 'em up for a day in my walk-in vault. Then I'll get hold of a bunch of these coin collector gentlemen that I know, and we can make some money on them. You see Terry," he went on excitedly now, "those coins are mint, they have never seen a pocket or a purse, you know what? I betcha I can get a hundred a piece for each one of those little double eagles. They haven't minted any in God knows how long, and they are going to be in big demand," he finished.

"Doesn't seem to be much discussion in what we are going to do with them then, does there?" I answered with a grin also as wide as Cochise Mountain. "And how about this Dave guy?" I asked. "Is he, see no evil, speak no evil."

"Oh yes," answered Hank, "or I wouldn't have him on the job. He never asks, I never offer to tell."

"Well it's 2 a.m., partner," said Hank, "we better catch some shut eye, big day tomorrow."

"Yes," I answered as I gestured towards the six duffel bags

of gold that were stacked up between our two tents. "I guess there is no sense in staying up to guard these from anyone."

"No I don't suppose so," admitted Hank, "the only ones that know anything about it is us and those two damned spooks."

"Hey, hey, partner," I laughed, "don't take their names in vain, we aren't on that chopper yet."

Hank grinned back, but I could detect a flicker of concern in those eyes of his.

Dave was as good as his word, we heard that old chopper coming before we had finished our second cup of coffee.

"I think he can set her down this morning," said Hank, "there's no wind and it was cooler yesterday."

And so it went. Dave set her down right in front of our tents and joined us in a cup of coffee.

Dave was now setting her down again in Hank's back yard in Phoenix. We hauled the gold on in, in Hank's garden wheelbarrow, and locked her up tight in the walk-in vault.

"Help yourself to the bar, partner," grinned old Hank, "you deserve it."

"Thanks, and compliment accepted," I told him, as I rummaged out another bottle of California white. I could hear Hank's voice on the telephone through his open office door.

"Yes, Brad," he was saying, "yes that's right, what I told you was right, I got $308,000 of the beautiful little devils. No you won't, no," he was laughing now. "No, Brad, not on a pig's ass you won't. Mint, mint," he echoed, "they have never seen pocket or purse. $75, no Brad, a thousand times no. Look I'm hanging up, if you want to go a hundred apiece and take the whole lot and caboodle then call us back, okay bye, Brad.

"Terry," he called. I went into the office and sat down in the armchair, sipping my California white.

"Old Brad from Palm Springs is going to take 'em all at a

hundred apiece. And a damned good deal for him too, he will double his money on some of them, if he waits and pokes around long enough. He hasn't said so yet but I know him, he will be calling back."

"It all sounds real good, partner," I said, "and it sure didn't take you long." No sooner had I finished the sentence than the desk phone rang to life.

"Hello, Hank here. Oh, is that you, Brad? What? Don't sell a damned thing, you want them all. Okay just a moment I have to consult my partner," he said. "Ter, that will be $154,000 apiece, I told him it would have to come in cash, is that all right with you?"

"That will be as good as it gets, Hank," I told him.

"Okay, Brad." He was shouting, "What? You're coming today with an armored van, okay do it any way you want to. Okay we will be here, okay bye, Brad. He's on his way, Ter, hired an armored courier both ways, should be here in three or four hours the way he gets in a hurry about these things. And he will be having the poor driver passing every thing between here and Palm Springs."

Brad arrived that evening, and was all smiles as the trade was made.

"Where in God's name did you find all of that beautiful stuff?" he asked Hank.

"The tooth fairy," answered Hank in his most authoritative tone.

"Must have had quite a mouthful of teeth," laughed Brad, and went on his way.

"What are you up to now, Terry?" Hank asked, as we split the pile of $1000 bank notes.

"Oh, I got to get back to Desert Hot Springs as soon as I can get a flight out," I told him.

He rummaged in his desk and came out with a flight

schedule. "Your next flight," he said, looking at his wristwatch, "leaves in 47 minutes, grab your stuff, we have just got time."

I stacked the $154,000 into a lock to your wrist briefcase that Hank had lent me, and we were on our way to the airport.

CHAPTER TWENTY-FOUR

FAREWELL TO CALIFORNIA

I took a cab from Palm Springs Airport, to my house in Desert Hot Springs. I locked the briefcase into the trunk of the Lincoln, thinking as I was doing it, *Got to find me a money laundry before too long*. The $149,000 that I had got from Ali was in there. Still in that briefcase that I had borrowed from Guy. Now this $154,000 brought it too $303,000. Also half the money for marriage that I had got from Ireene was still in there. Making it a total of $313,000. *California truly is the "Golden State,"* I joked to myself as I slam locked the trunk lid.

That good old California sun was coming up over the easterly rim of the desert, as I made my loop of the sand dune mountain on my morning's run. I showered and was enjoying my coffee out on the front porch when I saw the moving and storage van coming in the driveway. They were going to clear my house out today and store my furniture, until whenever.

The roadrunners began chirping, like the good little watchdogs that they were.

"Take everything, boys," I told the movers, "some of my personals are on my back, and the rest are in my car."

They got on the job and began lugging things out to the truck. My watchdogs were chirping loudly again. I looked down the driveway and this time it was Fat Billy the Roofer. He climbed out of the pickup with his usual outgoing smile, as wide as Desert Hot Springs.

"Top of the morning to you, Billy."

"Same to you," he answered. I could tell by his impatience that there was something really bugging him, and I also knew what it was. Fat Billy was afraid that he was missing something.

"Where the hell did you and that little Hank guy get to?" he asked with big expectant eyes. "I came by here for five days looking for you, saw that your car was here, that's when I realized that you guys had probably gone in the jeep. Where the hell did you two go? How long have you been back?"

"Slow down, Billy," I said, "everything is under control, we went on, let's call it a little mission, into Arizona. And I just got back last night."

Seeing that this was as far as I was going to elaborate on the subject, his next question was, "Where you off to now, Ter?"

"Well," I told him, "Mother Nature has started her old habit of bringing out the frying pan. And that's when her and I don't see eye to eye. So needless to say, I'm on the exodus for cooler pastures."

"Big Bear again?" he asked.

"No, not this time, Billy," I told him, this old boy's on his way home."

"What you mean Canada?" he asked, and didn't give me a chance to answer. "I thought that you were wanted up there, they are going to throw you in jail, aren't they?"

"I don't know what they are going to do, Billy," I answered him thoughtfully. "But I figure with a good store bought lawyer on my side, income tax evasion can't be that serious, if you have the money to pay them what they want."

"Maybe not, well maybe not," the fat boy muttered.

"When are you going?"

"Right now," I answered, "I have to go up to Big Bear and take care of my motor home, and then on to Canada."

"I'm sure going to miss you," said Billy, now seeing how serious I was. "A good thing I came up here," he went on, "or I wouldn't have seen you at all."

"Oh yes, you would have, Billy," I assured him, "I was going to stop at your place to say goodbye and to give you this little going away present."

I reached into my vest pocket and handed him a brown manila envelope, addressed to Mr. Bill Mcphee. And underneath the name I had scrawled:

Don't open until I am out of sight.

He stuffed the envelope into his shirt pocket and stood there misty-eyed, staring at me. I said, "Come on, Billy, get that damned old truck out of my way, I've got places to go."

He never spoke after that, just came over to me and gave me a great big bear hug, turned and drove away. I watched him go, realizing that I would never have a better friend, or a better playmate, anywhere in this world.

As I pulled out of Desert Hot Springs, I felt a little sad as I knew that I wouldn't be seeing it again for a long time, maybe never. I thought about Fat Billy the Roofer, and all of the dead in the water contracts that he had written up. And wondered just how long his luck would run, and what eventually would become of him. The envelope that I had given him, contained a letter telling how much I appreciated all of the good times that we had shared.

I had slipped a $1000 dollar bill inside the letter, as I knew that he was always short of money, and I figured this at least would give him a few days peace of mind. And the reason that I had scrawled, "don't open until I am out of sight," on the envelope, was for the reason that I was afraid if he opened it and read the letter, he would probably start his blubbering and crying. And I didn't want any of that, I'm just not built for it.

My trip up Big Bear Mountain's east pass went quickly and smoothly. It seemed like no time at all that I was pulling into the Crazy Horse parking lot. Also knowing that I wouldn't be seeing this place for a long time either, or possibly never, I walked very slowly across the parking lot so as to soak up as much memory as I could. The old saloon door was wide open as usual, and an old hit from Johnny Rivers came drifting out, "Memphis." A big hit for Johnny in the mid sixties.

"Welcome back," grinned old Guy from across the bar, as he handed me a cold Bud.

"Here for the summer now?" he asked.

"No," I said, and felt that sadness in me again, "just passing through this time, Guy."

"Where the hell are you off to now?" he asked.

"Going home this time," I told him.

"Not back to Canada?" he asked in surprise.

"Afraid so," I answered, "the time has come."

"When you coming back?" was his next question.

"It will be awhile, buddy," I answered, "but I'll be back, you can count on it."

"Well I hope so," he grinned, "gets kind of boring around here without you."

I finished my bottle of bud. We shook hands, I turned and walked out, never looking back…

THE END

Printed in the United States
112003LV00002B/47/A

9 781413 703627